“You

under

away. The more he’d thought about it in the past twenty-four hours, the more he really wanted her to say yes to his idea.

Ben backed the SUV out of the space and headed for the exit that would take them to downtown Blackwater Lake.

“Is there a reason we’re not going to Fireside here at the lodge?” she asked.

He glanced over at her and smiled at her expression. “Yes. My criteria for tonight is a locals favorite because it’s always busy.”

“I haven’t agreed to this insane charade yet.”

“I’m aware of that. But I think I can win you over.”

“Pretty confident, aren’t you?”

“Power of positive thinking.” He grinned at her. “Plus whatever your decision, being seen together will keep everyone off balance and that can’t hurt.”

“By ‘everyone’ you mean women.”

“Men talk, too.” He parked and shut off the ignition, then got out and walked around to open the passenger door.

Dear Reader,

When Dr. Ben McKnight returns home to Blackwater Lake he has a problem most guys would love to have—women won't leave him alone. They fake injuries to see him at the clinic, and others, including his own sister, try to fix him up. Apparently females think it's his duty to date, but that's no excuse for disrupting his medical practice. He's desperate to make it stop and comes up with a plan to make everyone believe he's off the dating market in order to be left alone. All he needs is a woman to go along with the idea.

Hotel heiress Camille Halliday has been sent to prove herself by reversing financial losses at her family's struggling property in remote Blackwater Lake. Though she's grown up and responsible now the whole town believes the bad press from her teenage indiscretions and everyone thinks she's too shallow, spoiled, short and blonde to be taken seriously. As if that's not bad enough, Ben asks her to be his pretend girlfriend. Call her crazy, but she's ready to try anything.

In exchange for participating in the charade, Ben will be her bridge to town acceptance and her employees' cooperation in making Blackwater Lake Lodge more profitable. He'll get peace and she'll have a pass to a better job in the big city of her choice. It's a simple win/win, but neither of them counts on the doctor's dating bargain turning into something as complicated as love.

I hope you enjoy!

Teresa Southwick

THE DOCTOR'S DATING BARGAIN

TERESA SOUTHWICK

ISBN-13: 978-0-373-65716-2

THE DOCTOR'S DATING BARGAIN

This edition published by arrangement with Harlequin Books S.A.

For questions and comments about the quality of this book, please contact us at CustomerService@Harlequin.com.

www.Harlequin.com

Printed in U.S.A.

Books by Teresa Southwick

Harlequin Special Edition

‡‡*To Have the Doctor's Baby* #2126
~~*Her Montana Christmas Groom* #2156
‡‡*Holding Out for Doctor Perfect* #2187
‡‡*The Doctor and the Single Mom* #2204
¤*The Maverick's Christmas Homecoming* #2230
¶¶*The Doctor's Dating Bargain* #2234

Silhouette Special Edition

The Summer House #1510
"Courting Cassandra"
Midnight, Moonlight & Miracles #1517
It Takes Three #1631
¶*The Beauty Queen's Makeover* #1699
At the Millionaire's Request #1769
§§*Paging Dr. Daddy* #1886
‡‡*The Millionaire and the M.D.* #1894
‡‡*When a Hero Comes Along* #1905
‡‡*Expecting the Doctor's Baby* #1924
‡*Marrying the Virgin Nanny* #1960
‡‡*The Doctor's Secret Baby* #1982
‡*The Nanny and Me* #2001
~*Taming the Montana Millionaire* #2059
‡‡*The Surgeon's Favorite Nurse* #2067
‡‡*Cindy's Doctor Charming* #2097

Silhouette Books

The Fortunes of Texas
Shotgun Vows

Silhouette Romance

**And Then He Kissed Me* #1405
**With a Little T.L.C.* #1421
The Acquired Bride #1474
**Secret Ingredient: Love* #1495
**The Last Marchetti Bachelor* #1513
***Crazy for Lovin' You* #1529
***This Kiss* #1541
***If You Don't Know by Now* #1560
***What If We Fall in Love?* #1572
Sky Full of Promise #1624
†*To Catch a Sheik* #1674
†*To Kiss a Sheik* #1686
†*To Wed a Sheik* #1696
††*Baby, Oh Baby* #1704
††*Flirting with the Boss* #1708
††*An Heiress on His Doorstep* #1712
§*That Touch of Pink* #1799
§*In Good Company* #1807
§*Something's Gotta Give* #1815

‡‡Men of Mercy Medical
‡The Nanny Network
§§The Wilder Family
*The Marchetti Family
**Destiny, Texas
†Desert Brides
††If Wishes Were…
§Buy-a-Guy
¶Most Likely To...
~Montana Mavericks: Thunder Canyon Cowboys
~~Montana Mavericks: The Texans are Coming!
¤Montana Mavericks: Back in the Saddle
¶¶Mercy Medical Montana

Other books by Teresa Southwick available in ebook format.

TERESA SOUTHWICK

lives with her husband in Las Vegas, the city that reinvents itself every day. An avid fan of romance novels, she is delighted to be living out her dream of writing for Harlequin.

To Maureen Child, Kate Carlisle, Christine Rimmer
and Susan Mallery, the best plot group ever!
Thanks for the friendship. And the fun. (Wine, too.)

Chapter One

"I'm in so much trouble."

Ben McKnight sat in the twilight shadows on the rear second-story deck of Blackwater Lake Lodge. The angry blonde who'd just stomped up the wooden stairs from the lush grounds below obviously was too caught up in her snit to notice him. She continued to mumble to herself as she paced back and forth in front of the redwood railing.

"Is it me?" she grumbled. "Do I attract trouble like black pants pick up pet hair? Or lint? Or fuzzballs? What is my problem?"

Then she lashed out with her foot and connected with one of the sturdy, upright posts anchoring the railing. It was a solid kick and after a few seconds the message traveled to her brain. When it got there, she blurted out, "Damn it! Now my foot's broken."

Beautiful, angry women who talked to themselves were not in Ben's wheelhouse, but broken bones he knew something about. He stood and walked out of the shadows into the circle of light cast by the property's perimeter lights.

"Maybe I can help."

She turned and gasped. "Good Lord, you startled me. Where the heck did you come from? I didn't know anyone was here."

"I figured that. The talking to yourself sort of gave it away."

"That happens when you don't want to talk to anyone else." She limped closer. "Who are you?"

"Ben McKnight. *Doctor* McKnight. I'm an orthopedic specialist at Mercy Medical Clinic."

"Call me crazy, but I didn't think it was in a doctor's job description to scare a person to death."

"True. *Do no harm* is the cornerstone of the Hippocratic Oath."

She pressed a hand to her chest and took a deep breath. "Then your bedside manner could use a little work, Doctor."

"Sorry." He watched her put weight on the foot and wince. "For the record, I don't recommend kicking things as a communication technique. Especially when you're wearing four-inch heels. Next time I'd use my words if I were you."

"What am I? Five?" The tone was full of irritation that seemed completely self-directed. "Okay. That was childish."

"Would you like me to take a look at the foot?"

"No. I'm fine. Completely over it. I'm calm and tranquil."

"I could tell," he said dryly. "All the pacing, stomping and trash talk were a clear indication that you're totally in your Zen place."

"I didn't mean for anyone to see that. It's been a bad

day and when that happens, I come up here to decompress. Pretty much every night. My serenity spot isn't normally occupied."

"Since I'm trespassing, the least I can do is listen." It would give him a chance to look at her mouth.

"Thanks, but I really have nothing to say."

"All evidence to the contrary. Look, whether or not you feel like talking, you should probably sit for a few minutes and elevate the foot. There could be swelling."

"Did you learn that in medical school?" She limped toward the two chairs nestled in the shadow of the lodge.

Ben put his hand under her elbow, mostly to help take some of her weight, but partly to touch her. "Actually, that's basic first aid. Every coach of every team I've been on since I was five has preached ice and heat for an injury."

"How many teams have you been on?"

She lowered herself into the Adirondack chair and leaned back with a sigh. There was a matching natural-wood ottoman and he cupped her ankle in his hand, then lifted it, resting it on the flat surface before slipping off her high-heeled shoe.

"A lot." Ben sat on the ottoman beside hers.

"What sports did you play?"

"Soccer. Basketball. Football. My senior year I was on the Blackwater Lake High School team that won state about fifteen years ago."

"So you're a local boy?"

"Yes."

"How come I haven't seen you around?" she asked.

"I just got back."

"Do you have family in Blackwater Lake?"

"Father. Older brother, younger sister."

"That qualifies." She thought for a moment. "So, I can't help being curious. You have family close by, which makes me wonder why you're sitting in the shadows on the deck all by yourself. Did you have a dinner date here at the lodge and she left in a huff? Are you a guest here at the hotel? Or just stalking someone who is a guest?"

He laughed. "I'm a guest. Staying here while I'm having a house built."

"Too old to live at home?"

"Something like that," he said.

The clouds drifted away from the moon and the deck was bathed in silver light, giving Ben a better view of the blonde. She was prettier than he'd thought, with a small face and deep dimples. Her eyes looked blue, although he couldn't tell the shade, and tilted up slightly at the corners. Her hair was straight, and cut in layers that framed her face and fell past her shoulders. Her arm through the light sweater she wore had felt delicate and small-boned. Although the heels gave the impression of height, she barely came up to his shoulder, which made her not so tall.

Suddenly he wondered who he was talking to. He didn't even know her name. On top of that, she was the one asking all the questions. "Are you sure you don't want to tell me why you're so ticked off?"

"There's nothing to say."

"For starters you could define the mess you're in."

"I was hoping you didn't hear that," she said.

"Nope. Sorry. Every word. And let me quote here, 'I'm in so much trouble.' Should I be afraid to get too close? Are you at the top of an assassination list? On the run from law enforcement? A CIA spy doing covert surveillance?"

"Right, because so much happens in Blackwater Lake that the government needs to surveil." There was a suggestion of sarcasm and the barest hint of mockery in her tone.

"You don't like it here?"

She met his gaze. "Let's just say it's not New York or L.A."

"So define trouble. You could be pregnant," he pointed out.

"You have quite the imagination." Her lips turned up at the corners in a brief show of amusement. She had an awfully spectacular mouth when it wasn't all pinched and tight. "And that would be a miracle since I haven't had sex in—"

"Yes?" He looked at her and waited.

"That's really none of your business."

"Maybe not, but now I'm awfully curious."

"Be that as it may," she said, "you're a stranger and I'm not in the habit of sharing personal information with someone I've barely met, Dr. McKnight."

"At least you know my name. That's more than I can say about you."

"Camille Halliday." She looked at him expectantly, as if waiting for recognition. Actually more like bracing for it, as if the information would be unpleasant.

The name did sound familiar, but he couldn't place it. "It's nice to meet you, Miss Halliday."

"Likewise, Dr. McKnight. Now, I really should be going." She slid the punting foot off the ottoman and gingerly tested it on the deck.

"How does it feel?"

"Several of my toes hurt," she admitted.

"Can you walk on it?"

"I have to. Work to do."

"At the hotel?"

"Yes."

"In what capacity?" he wanted to know.

"I run the place."

That's when her last name clicked. Her family had made

a fortune in the hotel and hospitality industry. "You're one of the Halliday hotel chain family."

"Among other things," she said a little mysteriously. After sliding her other leg off the ottoman, she moved forward in the chair and tested more weight on the foot. Drawing in a breath she said, "That smarts a little."

Ben realized he didn't want her to leave yet. "I'd be happy to look at it for you. Sometimes taping a couple toes together helps."

"Thanks for the tip. Taping a toe I can handle." Her words implied there was a whole lot more she couldn't handle.

"Okay. But if you don't want me to examine it, at least sit for a few more minutes and take the pressure off."

She sighed, then nodded. "I can sit, but that won't relieve any pressure."

"You're not talking about the foot now, are you?"

"No." She caught the corner of her bottom lip between her top teeth as she stared out over the back grass and the thick evergreen trees beyond.

"What's wrong? Might help to get it off your chest."

"It might, but I can't. One of the first things I learned getting a master's degree in hotel management was never unburden yourself to a guest."

"I'm not really a guest," he said. "It's more like a lease until my house is ready."

"Why didn't you do that?" she asked. "Rent a place, I mean?"

"Oh, so you get to ask questions but I don't? How about a quid pro quo?" He met her gaze. "You tell me about your trouble and I'll spill about my living arrangements. What can it hurt?"

She stared at him for several moments, then nodded. "It's pretty common knowledge that this property in the hotel chain isn't doing well financially. My father gave me six months to stop Blackwater Lake Lodge from hemorrhaging money or he'll close it down."

"I see. So you have half a year."

"Not anymore." She blew out a breath. "I've been here two and a half months. The employees are intractable and do their own thing. Personnel turnover is too high and we bleed money in training until a new hire is competent enough to pull their own weight. I think someone is skimming money from the books, but I'm so busy putting out fires that I can't get to the bottom of it. And I'm running out of time."

"Do you have a personal attachment to this property?"

"I'd never seen it until January." She sighed. "But my father is testing me. If I can pull this off, I'll get a choice assignment somewhere that's not in the wilderness of Montana."

"Ah." Making the lodge successful was her ticket out of here.

Ben could understand. Once upon a time he couldn't wait to shake the dirt, mud and mountain air off, but he didn't feel that way now.

"So, why are you back here?" she asked.

"To build a house and put down roots. Blackwater Lake is a great place to live." When she stood, he did, too. "Can't see renting something, settling in, then moving again. I'm focused on expanding Mercy Medical Clinic and providing quality health care for the town and the tourists who come here to visit."

"It's a really noble goal." She touched his arm to steady herself while slipping her shoe back on, then limped toward the stairs. At the top she turned and said, "Good luck with that, Doctor. Now I really have to say good-night."

After she disappeared from sight, he heard her uneven step as she walked down the stairs.

Ben found her intriguing and was sorry she'd had to leave. Still, the quid pro quo had put everything in perspective. He was staying and her objective was to get out of town as fast as possible.

That was too bad.

Until last night Camille hadn't known Ben McKnight existed and now she wondered how he could have been staying in her hotel without her being aware. He was tall, funny and as good-looking as any man she'd met in L.A. or New York, and she'd met a lot of men, according to every rag sheet tabloid paper on the planet.

Now Dr. Ben McKnight was having dinner in the Blackwater Lake Lodge restaurant where she was filling in as hostess. The last one had quit and it was hard to run a five-star establishment without a greeter and seater. Hopefully the interviews she had tomorrow would be productive. Fortunately it was Sunday and not busy. At least it hadn't been until Doctor Do-Good had arrived and asked for a table by himself.

Since then at least four women, two from the lodge staff and two civilians, had come in, sat with him, written something down on a small piece of paper, then handed it to him. Since they were small scraps of paper, she was pretty sure the information wasn't their medical history.

At the moment he was sitting by himself and the place was practically empty except for a couple lingering over coffee and dessert at their table near the stone fireplace.

Cam just couldn't stop herself. She strolled over to where she'd seated him a little while ago and smiled. "Did you enjoy your dinner, Doctor?"

Ben nodded. "I did. The food here is excellent."

"Amanda will appreciate hearing that. She's the chef." And someone Cam had coaxed here from New York. The plan was to prove herself in six months and the two of them would get their pick of prime assignments in one of the Halliday Hospitality Corporation's other properties. "Can I get you something from the bar?"

"No, thanks. I'm on call for the clinic."

"Are you expecting broken bones tonight?"

"Mercy Medical Clinic docs rotate the responsibility of being available to triage emergency calls."

"Excuse me?"

"We take information and decide if the patient on the phone needs to see a doctor and which one could best take care of them. If it's an orthopedic problem, I'm their guy. Otherwise Adam Stone, the family practice specialist, is up."

Cam was "up" all day and night here at the lodge. It wasn't the same as life and death, but she had to be available to deal with any crisis situation. Her performance was being evaluated, and Dean Halliday, her father and president of Halliday Hospitality, didn't grade on a curve.

"Maybe dessert and coffee?" she suggested. "I happen to know the chef makes the best seven-layer chocolate cake in Montana."

"Is that a fact?" Dark brown eyes teased and taunted.

"Slight exaggeration. But if it's not the best you've tasted in Blackwater Lake, this meal is on the house."

"Can you afford to take the chance, what with losing money and all? Or," he added, "I could lie just to get the meal comped."

"You could."

It wouldn't be the first time a man had lied and taken advantage of her, but she'd been younger then. Naive. Vulnerable. All of that was a pretty way of saying she'd been stupid and her judgment about men sucked. But she was going to prove herself here in this little backwater town or die trying.

She gave him her best smile, the one that showed off her dimples. "But if you don't tell the truth, we'll both know."

"You're on." He laughed and showed off his own considerable charms.

His teeth were very white and practically perfect. The pretty people she'd once counted as her closest friends all had cosmetic work to make their smiles perfect, but Ben's looked like nothing more than good genes. There were streaks in his brown hair that came from the sun and not a bottle at the salon and the bump in his nose kept him from being too pretty. He had a natural ruggedness about him that had nothing to do with acting technique and everything to do with being a manly man. Again with the good genes.

Cam had promised herself after a teenage run-in with police that she'd never again do anything she'd regret. Last night she broke that pledge. She regretted not letting Dr. Ben McKnight examine her foot. Not because she needed anything more medical than an aspirin and a bag of frozen peas for swelling, but simply to feel his big, competent hands on her leg.

Focus, she told herself. Glancing around, she saw Jenny, the lone waitress tonight, and signaled her over. The server shot her a dirty look, then moved to the table and smiled warmly at the doctor.

"What can I get you, Dr. McKnight?"

"Miss Halliday has talked me into a cup of coffee and a piece of Montana's best chocolate cake."

"Excellent choice," Jen said. "I'll bring it right out."

"I should walk back and get it myself," he said. "It's going to add an extra mile to my run in the morning."

"You look fine to me." Jenny smiled and there was definite flirtatious eyelash-batting going on.

Cam held in a sigh and made a mental note to add an item to the staff meeting agenda. Friendly, but not too friendly. It was a fine line.

She looked down at the customer and gave him her professional, but not too friendly smile. "You may have to run an extra mile, but I promise the cake will be worth it." Then she turned away.

"You're leaving?"

"I have work to do."

"Is the place that busy? Can you keep me company?"

"From what I saw you had plenty of company during dinner, Doctor."

He shrugged. "People in Blackwater Lake are friendly."

"Is it just me or merely a coincidence that all those friendly Blackwater Lake people were of the female persuasion?"

"Are you jealous, Miss Halliday?"

"What if I were, Dr. McKnight?"

"I'd be flattered," he said.

"And I'd have a target on my back. Enjoy your dessert," she said, turning away.

"Whoa, not so fast, Cam. Do you mind if I call you that?" Without waiting for an answer he pointed to the chair at a right angle to his. "It's just plain mean to make a cryptic remark like that, then walk away."

"I have no reason to stay."

"Aren't you supposed to be friendly to your guests?" he asked.

"The first rule of hospitality," she confirmed. "And I have been. But there's a line that shouldn't be crossed."

"Isn't the customer always right?"

"Yes, but—"

"So, sit. Take a load off that foot." He looked down at her legs in four-inch heels. "Nice shoes. How is the foot, by the way?"

"Fine." She didn't take him up on the offer to sit because that wasn't professional. But she didn't leave, either.

"Tell me about the target on your back."

"Obviously you were smart enough to pass medical school. Do you really not get it?" That was tough to believe. A man as good-looking as he had to have had opportunities. He'd probably left this small town for college a naive guy of eighteen, but surely he'd been around the block a time or two since then. "You're quite a catch."

"What am I? A fish?" The twinkle in his eyes said he knew where this was going and wasn't the least offended.

That was fortunate because in the hospitality game one always aimed to please. "You're a doctor and not hard on the eyes—"

"Did you just say I'm cute?"

"I said the women in this tiny little town might perceive you that way and you probably make a decent living as a doctor."

"Are you asking?" He rested his forearms on the white-cloth-covered table.

"I'm not interested. But clearly a number of women are. A single guy—" She stopped as a thought struck her. "You aren't married, are you?"

"Nope."

"Divorced?"

"One would have to have been married for that to be the case."

"So you've never been married."

Before Camille could continue the line of questioning, Jenny brought over his cake and the assistant waiter delivered a saucer and cup, then filled it with coffee.

"Anything else I can do for you?" Jenny asked.

"No. But thanks." Ben gave her a smile.

The waitress returned it and moved behind him where she leveled Cam with a look that if it could kill would render her a rust-colored stain on the floor.

Ben forked off a piece of cake then put it in his mouth, his eyes never leaving hers. After chewing and swallowing, the sound of pleasure he made was almost sexual. Since her January arrival in this state that was so close to Canada, she'd never once been too warm. Not until now. And she very much wanted to fan herself.

Steady, girl. What were they talking about? Oh, right. He'd never been married.

"What's wrong with you?" she asked.

"Excuse me? I believe I just proved your point about this being the best cake in Montana."

"I'm not talking cake." She folded her arms over her chest. "You're handsome, smart, a doctor who returned to his hometown to practice medicine. Approximately thirty-five—"

"Close," he confirmed. "Thirty-four."

"Apparently I'm out of practice. And don't interrupt me. I'm on a roll. You're thirty-four, not married and never been married. What's wrong with you?"

"Am I gay, you mean?"

"That's not what I asked, but—"

"No. I'm not."

"That's a relief." She realized that thought hadn't stayed in her head and added, "I mean, for the single women in Blackwater Lake who went to all the trouble of giving you their phone numbers."

"How do you know that?"

"I've been watching them hand you slips of paper too

small to be a résumé or autobiographical novel. And I did catch a glimpse of numbers."

"You're very observant."

"Attention to detail is the hallmark of the hospitality business," she said, irritated at how much she sounded like her father. "So, how does someone who looks so good on paper escape personal entanglements unscathed?"

The twinkle in his eyes vanished and the warm cocoa color turned almost black. "Who says I did?"

"So you have a story." It wasn't a question.

"Doesn't everyone? You go first."

"Nice try." She shook her head.

If he was curious he could just Google her. There was plenty documented on the internet that she'd never live down no matter how hard she tried. Or he could ask the hotel staff. They'd be happy to share.

And judge. The employees had made up their minds about her based on tabloid stories and entertainment gossip. They'd decided she was too shallow, too spoiled, too short and too blonde to be taken seriously.

Why should Ben McKnight be any different?

Chapter Two

"I don't think it's broken, but I'll know for sure after I look at the X-ray."

"The garage is really busy right now so I'm holding you to that not-broken thing."

Ben hadn't expected to start the week treating anyone in his family, but he had been wrong. Sydney McKnight sat on the paper-covered exam table cradling her right hand. His little sister was a pretty, brown-eyed brunette who loved fixing cars as much as he liked fixing people. As a little girl she'd followed their father around McKnight's Automotive and learned from the best mechanic in Montana.

"You know," he said, "if you wanted some big brother time, we could have done lunch. It would have been a lot less painful for you."

"Not if you made me buy." She winced as he probed the swelling. "In my opinion, what this clinic really needs is a neurologist. You need to have your head examined, find out why it's so big."

"Seriously, Syd. This is nasty. What happened?"

"An accident at the garage." She shrugged. "There was a wrench involved. My hand slipped. Occupational hazard."

"And aren't you lucky big brother the doctor is back to take care of you?"

"We've done all right."

Without you, he thought. Ben knew she hadn't meant to make him feel guilty for leaving, but he did anyway. His father had encouraged him to do what was necessary for his future the same way he'd nurtured Sydney's love affair with cars. Eventually Ben had gone, but now he was back. Where he wanted to be.

The exam room door opened and nurse Ginny Irwin walked in. She was in her late fifties and had blue eyes that missed nothing. Her silver hair was cut in a short, no-fuss style. It suited her no-nonsense attitude.

"Hey, Syd," she said.

"Hi, Ginny." His sister started to lift her hand in greeting, then winced and lowered it.

"I've emailed the X-rays to the radiologist at the hospital and it will be a while before we get the report. But here are the films, Ben." Ginny had known him since he was a kid and didn't feel the need to address him as *Doctor*.

He liked that. Adding *Doctor* to his name didn't make him a better medical practitioner. No polite protocols or assembly-line medicine, just solid personal care to, sometimes literally, get people back on their feet.

"Let's take a look." He put the films on the lighted view box. He wasn't a radiologist, but in his expert opinion there was no break, although he took his time studying all the small bones, just to be sure.

"Don't keep me in suspense," Syd said.

"I have to look at the full range of densities. It can go from white to black and I need to evaluate the contrast ratio for a diagnosis."

"Please don't go all medical techno-speak on me," Sydney begged.

"It's not broken."

"Good." Ginny almost smiled, then looked sternly at the patient. "I don't want to see you back in here, Sydney Marie."

"Yes, ma'am. I'd salute, but this Pillsbury Doughboy hand would just punish me."

"In so many ways. Take care," Ginny said, just before slipping out the door.

"She scares me," his sister said. "So I'll ask you. Can I go back to work?"

"Really?" He folded his arms over his chest. "I'm the weak link? Do we need to get Ginny back in here to keep you in line, Sydney Marie?"

"I'm happy to stay in line if you'll just tell me what I have to do so I can get back to work."

"Take the rest of the day off. Use ice and over-the-counter pain meds. When the swelling goes down you can work."

"That's it? You're not going to do anything? No quick fix? What kind of doctor are you?"

"The kind who replaces hips and fixes broken bones, sometimes with surgery. I have a piece of paper that says it's okay for me to do that."

"Just asking. I guess you'll come in handy for water- and snow-skiing seasons." She settled her injured hand on her thigh. "Speaking of that…how do you like living at Blackwater Lake Lodge?"

The mention of his living arrangement turned his thoughts to the lady who was in charge of the place where he lived. This wasn't the first time she'd crossed his mind and every time it happened, the thought was followed by a vague regret that she wouldn't be around very long.

"Did I say something wrong?" Syd's eyes narrowed.

"What? No. Why?"

"You look funny."

"Define funny," he said.

"I don't know. Sort of goofy. Sappy. Like you walked down the hall at Blackwater Lake High and saw the girl you had a crush on."

"Interesting diagnosis, Doctor."

"Am I right about a woman being involved?" she persisted.

"Yes."

"I'd clap my hands in excitement, but..." She looked ruefully at the puffy extremity. "Who is she? Anyone I know?"

"Do you know Camille Halliday?"

"Everyone knows her." Syd's expression said it wasn't in a good way. "She's the hotel heiress."

"I know. Met her Saturday." And he'd seen her again at dinner last night. He wondered if she was having another bad day.

"Are you aware that she has a certain reputation?"

"What kind of rep?"

"Partying. Hanging with a wild crowd. Name always in the paper and not for sending mosquito nets to Africa to wipe out malaria. She even went to jail. Although they let her out early."

"Good behavior?"

"Overcrowding," Syd answered. "You didn't know about this stuff?"

"No."

"Have you been living under a rock?"

Sort of. "Las Vegas is surrounded by rocky mountains and rocks are frequently used for landscaping, what with water being scarce in the desert. But none of that qualifies as living under one."

Unless you counted working too hard to think about anything else. Now he had time to wonder about Camille Halliday. What his sister just said didn't fit the ambitious, hardworking woman he'd met. "Was this jail thing recent?"

"No. She was in her teens."

Ah. "And where did you get all this unimpeachable information?"

"The tabloids." Syd grinned shamelessly. "I love to read them. A guilty pleasure."

"Then here's a headline for you. Don't believe everything you read." He slid his fingers into the pockets of his white lab coat. "I found Cam to be bright, funny, focused and a serious businesswoman. Sexy, too."

His sister's eyes narrowed. "Do you have the hots for her?"

No. Maybe. Irrelevant. "She's got her sights set on bigger and better things. Blackwater Lake Lodge is where she's proving herself. She can't wait to move up the career ladder, preferably to a city with a more impressive population."

Syd's dark eyes gleamed with plans he knew he wouldn't like. "That's a relief."

"Why?"

"Here's the thing. You're not getting any younger, Ben."

"Yeah. I think they taught us that in med school," he said dryly.

"No. Seriously. You should think about settling down."

"I'm building a house. Doesn't that count?"

"Good start." She shifted her tush on the table and the

disposable paper rustled. "You should think about a woman to go along with it. And I just happen to have some suggestions."

His sister and every other female in this town had ideas. There'd been matchmaking vibes since he'd touched down. Even Cam had noticed women giving him their phone numbers. "Why am I not surprised?"

Syd ignored his sarcasm. "Annie Higgins is pretty and fun."

"Isn't she divorced with three kids?"

"So?" His sister obviously saw the negative in his expression because she moved on. "Okay. Darlene Litsey has never been married. She has a great personality."

"Personality? Isn't that code for a deal-breaking flaw?"

"Maybe she's a little controlling," Syd admitted. "Okay. I've got the perfect woman for you."

A vision of Cam Halliday flashed into his mind. Specifically her expression when he'd eaten the sinfully good cake. He'd have sworn it was a look of pure lust, but that could just be wishful thinking.

"Are you paying attention?" Syd demanded.

"I'm all ears."

She eyed him critically. "They are a little big. I wasn't going to say anything...but you're a doctor. Surely there's something you can do to fix them."

"Very funny. Now that I think about it, what woman would want to go out with Dumbo?"

"Don't sell yourself short. You've got a lot to offer." She did that critical appraisal thing again. "Handsome, in spite of the ears. Funny, except to me. And you're a doctor."

Cam had said almost the same thing last night. "So?"

"A woman wants to be taken care of. Goes back to caveman days. Picking the biggest, strongest Neanderthal/

Cro-Magnon who can hunt, gather and beat the crap out of anyone who tries to take what's his."

"None of that pertains to me," he protested.

"Sure it does. Modern man just pays people to do all of the above and you can pay better than most. I happen to know you got a couple of bucks when you sold your practice in Las Vegas."

"You could say that."

When he finished medical training, Ben had researched areas of the country for a place to practice medicine. Las Vegas was booming and there was a scarcity of doctors in his field. He set up an office, built a solid reputation all over the valley, hired more doctors to make the business end of it more lucrative, then sold it to the partners. The deal made him a millionaire and wise investments had more than doubled his net worth. He never had to work again if he didn't want to.

Except he loved what he did. Long hours and hard work had earned him the freedom to use his knowledge to help people without having to practice cookie-cutter medicine. He could take his time and give patients the personal attention he wanted to.

"Ben, Emily Decatur is really nice."

"I remember her from high school. She works at the Lodge."

"Right. And you live there. It's a sign. It's convenient."

Cam Halliday worked where he lived, too, and somehow that seemed more convenient to him. "I'm sure Emily is great, but there's no spark."

"Three strikes and you're out. I just provided you with a list of perfectly lovely women and you found something wrong with every one." Syd's frustration was showing. "If you don't want a woman, why did you come home?"

"I'm not sure those two statements actually go together."

"They do in my mind. Las Vegas has a bigger dating pool than Blackwater Lake, so why are you here?"

"Believe it or not, dating isn't my reason for coming back."

"I get it." She was angry and frustrated in equal parts. "You're not looking at all. This is about Judy Coulter, isn't it?"

"My main squeeze in high school and college." After that not so much.

"Yeah. The same one who strung you along for years then married some ski bum she'd only known a month. And moved back East with."

All of that was true and it hurt at the time. But he'd gotten over her a long time ago. "She did me a favor, Syd."

"She broke your heart. How is that a good thing?"

"She didn't break my heart. When I started med school there were no distractions. I put all my energy into school and becoming the best doctor possible."

"You are pretty good," she grudgingly admitted.

"I thank Judy for that."

His sister frowned. "If you were really the best, you'd make my hand better right now."

"Only time can do that," he said gently.

"Speaking of time and healing, I just thought of someone else for the dating list—"

"Stop. I've barely unpacked."

"Oh, pooh," she scoffed. "It's been a couple weeks. You have a duty to date someone."

Now he was getting frustrated. "Right back at you, sis. Who are you going out with? Do I know the guy?"

"I'm taking a break from men."

"Why?"

"I don't want to talk about it."

There was a story. Ben saw it in her eyes, but wouldn't

push. If he set a good example, maybe she'd back off, too. "Okay. So you understand where I'm coming from."

"Not really. You've had a very long break," she started.

He barely held back a groan. She was like a bulldog with a favorite bone. How long would it take before she decided to let this go? He wasn't opposed to dating, just wanted to do it in his own time, his own way.

He would go out when he met someone who intrigued him as much as Camille Halliday.

With a four-inch heel in each hand, Cam walked out of the bedroom into her suite's sitting area. All the bigger, more expensive lodge rooms were on the top floor and she liked living here a lot. It was big, a convenient distance to work and the mattress was soft and comfy. Love seats covered in earth-tone stripes faced each other in front of the fireplace. There was a small kitchen and a cherrywood table in the dining area.

She stopped in front of the mirror over a small table in the entryway for a last check on her appearance before starting the day.

"Hair?" She nodded with satisfaction. "Check."

Something about the water here in Montana brought out the best in her shoulder-length layered style.

"Makeup? Check." It was flawless. She had the money to buy good skin care products and cosmetics and had paid big bucks for a professional makeup artist to teach her the techniques for perfect application.

"Clothes? Dressed for success." She loved this lavender suit with the pencil skirt and fitted matching jacket. The heels matched perfectly.

"It's Tuesday," she reminded herself. "Maybe today I'll get staff cooperation. And maybe I'll flap my arms and fly to the moon."

All those power of positive thinking seminars had been a waste of time for this exile in Blackwater Lake. So far the information and methods hadn't achieved any measurable real-life results.

She was about to slip her heels on when shouting in the hallway shattered the silence in her room. "It's too early for this," she groaned. "Rocky and Apollo Creed couldn't make it just one day without going a couple of rounds?"

Cam opened her door and hurried into the carpeted hall barefoot. Patty Evans and Crystal Ames, a housekeeping team on the staff, stood two inches apart, shouting into each other's faces. They were in their early thirties and about the same height, which made them quite a bit taller than Cam, but she couldn't spare the time for her shoes.

She tried to get between them, but they pretty much ignored her. "Ladies, this is unprofessional."

"Stop flirting with him." Patty's hair curved under in a brown bob. She wore the black pants and gray, fitted smock shirt that was the department uniform.

A honey blonde, Crystal had her hair held back with a big clip. "I wasn't flirting. Just being friendly. You're paranoid." She waved her index finger in the other woman's direction. "And you need your head examined."

"There's nothing wrong with my head," Patty retorted. "I know what I saw. You always want what's mine."

"You're imagining things." Crystal moved even closer.

Patty lifted her chin defensively. "Stay away from Scooter."

Someone named Scooter was worth coming to blows? Cam had to break this up. The most expensive lodge rooms were nearby. Unprofessional behavior like this was inappropriate anywhere, but especially here. Social media being what it was, negative information could go viral on the internet and she had enough problems without that.

"Ladies—" She put a hand on each of their shoulders and used gentle pressure to move them back an inch or two. "That will be enough."

Patty's blue eyes blazed. "It's not nearly enough. Not until she backs off my boyfriend."

"How many times do I have to say this? I'm not coming on to him." Crystal jammed her hands on her hips. "You've got quite an imagination. Get over it."

"Stop it." Cam raised her voice which she hated to do, but a sharp slap to snap them out of it wasn't an option. "This is unacceptable—"

A door opened behind them. "Hi."

Cam held in a groan. It was only one word, but she knew that deep voice. Before she could turn and respond, the two housekeepers relaxed their combative body language.

"Hey, Ben." Patty smiled. "I heard you were back in town and staying here."

"It's been a while." Ben was wearing surgical scrub pants with a long-sleeved white shirt beneath the matching shapeless blue top. "How are you, Patty? Crystal?"

The blonde flashed him a flirty smile. "Fine. How've you been?"

"Good. It's great to be back."

"We should get together for a drink and catch up."

He nodded. "After work some time."

"Sounds good." Patty looked at her partner. "Speaking of that, we've got to get busy."

"Right. Catch you later, Ben."

"Have a good one." He returned their wave before the two women moved down the hall to where the housekeeping cart was pushed against the wall.

"I'm sorry you had to see that," Cam said.

"I actually didn't see anything. Hearing is a different

story." He leaned a shoulder against the doorjamb that was right next to hers. "Are you still in trouble?"

"Tip of the iceberg. Those two are on a very long list of employees who do their own thing."

"So, that's a yes to trouble?" His dark eyes sparkled with humor, no doubt the memory of the other night on the deck.

"It is," she admitted.

"Are you going to kick something?" When he looked down at her bare feet, his gaze turned decidedly, intensely sexy and suggestive.

"No. It was a lesson. I'll use my words. Right after I get my shoes." Every time she saw him it felt like a power struggle and she didn't like feeling at a disadvantage. She also didn't like the little shimmy in her heart when his eyes went all hot and smoldery. That couldn't be good. "I have to get to work."

"Don't let me keep you."

She nodded, then looked up. "And Ben?"

"Hm?"

"I'd consider it a personal favor if you forgot about the little disagreement. I really am sorry you had to see that and I intend to talk to them." For the umpteenth time. If only she could promise him it wouldn't happen again.

Ben glanced down the empty hall where the two women had been. "I take it Patty and Crystal don't get along?"

There was no point in denying what he'd just witnessed for himself. "I referee practically on a daily basis." Then his words sank in. "You know their names."

"We went to high school together."

"I see." Small-town life, she reminded herself. "They're good at their jobs. When not arguing."

"Those two haven't gotten along since Crystal stole

Patty's boyfriend before prom and she missed the highlight of high school."

Cam wouldn't know. Her teen years had been erratic and traditional school wasn't in her frame of reference. "That's good information."

"I've noticed that housekeepers here at the lodge work in teams."

"It's efficient."

He nodded. "I know what you said about personnel turnover and the cost of training. Obviously you feel it's important to retain those two. So it might be a good idea to split them up."

"It crossed my mind, but I've been working in—what did you call it? Triage? Dealing with the most important things first. Operating in crisis mode."

The longer Cam stood looking up at him, the more she noticed how handsome he was. How easy he was to talk to. How good he smelled. How safe he made her feel.

That was something she hadn't felt since losing her big brother when he was only nineteen. Since then men had come on to her, using her to get their name in the paper. Famous by association. But there was something trustworthy about Ben.

He folded his arms over his chest. "You should be used to crisis mode."

His voice was pleasant and teasing, but her stomach dropped at the words. It had been too much to hope for. "Why?"

"Your tabloid history is pretty colorful."

"So you know about that."

"I Googled you."

"That's a lot of information to wade through." Disappointment sat like a stone in her gut.

"Not so much after you went to jail."

It was hard, but she managed not to wince. She would never be able to erase her infamous past and the lies that were part of it. She knew the truth and could set the record straight, but she couldn't make him believe it.

"Being in a cell, even segregated from the general population, was more scary than I can tell you. I was grateful for early release and determined not to go back. Ever. I returned to college."

"Coincidentally, that was about the time all the stories dried up."

"Photographers still stalked me, waiting for a screwup to document and sell papers. But I was more determined to get an education and have a career. Accomplish something. Do more than be famous for being famous."

"Good for you."

Right. The words sounded supportive, but she knew better. Everyone wanted something.

"I really have to get to work," she said.

"Me, too." He straightened and looked down at her. "I'd like to see you later."

"That's not a good idea." The door to her suite was right next to his and she headed for it now. Over her shoulder she said, "Have a wonderful day."

In her room she leaned against the closed door and dragged in air. Since college the nice guys had shunned her. Classes, studying and getting exemplary grades were all she had. The loneliness and isolation hurt deeply, but she'd learned valuable lessons. She needed a solid, successful career because that would be all she had, all she could count on.

It was time to focus on that career. Making Blackwater Lake Lodge into a lucrative property in the family hotel chain was her ticket out of this town. It would get her away from the handsome, sexy doctor who was nothing more than another nice guy who wouldn't want to bring her home to meet his family.

Chapter Three

Ben McKnight had never pictured himself as a Chamber of Commerce sort of guy, but here he was at the monthly Blackwater Lake meeting. He'd been interested in hearing Mayor Loretta Goodson's plans for growing the community, expanding Mercy Medical Clinic and eventually building a hospital here in town. Being in on that project from the beginning was one of the reasons he'd come back. Blending the best and newest medicine with a small-town, hands-on approach was exciting and rewarding.

Apparently he wasn't the only one interested in long-term planning. It was a standing-room-only crowd in the council chamber here at City Hall.

"I think we've thoroughly covered all the information about the architect hired to draw up the plans for the Mercy Medical Clinic expansion. The town council and I liked the work she showed us, but she also has the lowest fee. McKnight Construction will be doing the building. Is there any further business or questions?" The mayor, an attractive woman who looked thirty but was probably ten years older, glanced around the room. Her shoulder-length, layered brown hair caught the overhead light as she turned her head. She smiled, but it didn't quite reach her gray eyes. "All right, seeing no raised hands, that concludes the meeting. There are refreshments in the back. Thank you for coming, everyone."

Almost instantly chair legs scraped and talking commenced as people stood and filed out of the room or to the table filled with coffee and dessert.

Ben had been at the clinic late setting a patient's broken arm and barely made it to the meeting. With no time to eat, he was starving. After grabbing a couple cookies and a brownie, he looked around. Against the wall he noticed Cabot Dixon, an old high school friend, talking to the pretty redhead who owned the marina store on the lake and was engaged to Adam Stone, the family-practice doctor at the clinic. He moved toward them and Cabot grinned.

"I heard you were back in town, Ben."

"Good to see you, Cab." He set his coffee on the seat of a chair and shook the other man's hand.

"Do you know Jill Beck?"

"I do. How's that little guy of yours?" Ben had met them at the clinic when they visited Adam at work.

"C.J. is great." Her blue eyes glowed with pride and pleasure. "Adam is keeping an eye on him tonight. Tyler's there, too."

"How old is that boy of yours, Cab?"

"Seven. Can't believe it. I remember when he was hardly bigger than my hand and I was trying to figure out which end to put the diaper on and which one to feed."

"You've done a great job," Jill said, "because he's healthy and happy."

"It was one day at a time, one crisis at a time." He shook his head at the memories. "Seems like yesterday he was a toddler."

"I look forward to seeing him. Preferably not at the clinic."

"From your mouth to God's ear," the man said fervently.

Ben knew Cabot had been married and his wife took off right after the baby's birth. Apparently, in addition to a husband and newborn son, small-town life wasn't her thing. And speaking of that… In his peripheral vision he noticed a flash of red. Camille Halliday was a few feet away from the refreshment table, by herself and holding a cup of coffee. She stood out like a fly in milk.

The people in this room were dressed in denim and flannel. Mayor Goodson had on a navy blue blazer with her jeans to negotiate the line between casual and professional. There was an occasional pair of khakis, and Ben was in scrubs, but that was as formal as anyone got.

Cam was wearing a stylishly short, snug skirt and fitted red jacket with a ruffle at the waist. Her four-inch red come-and-get-me heels made her legs look longer than he thought they were and shapely enough to make his fingers tingle to know for sure.

Jill must have noticed where he was looking. "Camille Halliday is prettier in person that she is in photographs."

"I'll have to take your word." Ben forced himself to look away. He took a chocolate chip cookie from his plate and bit into it. After chewing and swallowing he said, "I've never seen pictures of her."

"Really?" The redhead looked surprised. "She's been all over magazines and tabloid news."

"I've been busy." He shrugged. "Barely put it together when I met her at the lodge. I'm staying there until I build my house."

"I'd steer clear of her." Cabot's eyes were dark with suspicion.

"Have you met her?"

"No. And that's fine with me."

"I can't help wondering what she's doing in Blackwater Lake." Jill sipped her coffee. "It's painfully obvious that she doesn't fit in here."

Ben noticed that people were looking curiously at her, but no one ventured over. She looked a little lost and the stubborn lift of her chin said she was trying not to be.

"I'm going to talk to her," he said.

"Bad idea." Cabot shook his head in warning.

"Why?"

"She's way out of your league."

"That would be a problem if I were looking for something serious." He already knew that was a waste of time, because the lady had her sights set on bigger and more high-profile than here. "But there's no harm in being friendly."

"Yes, there is." His friend looked like he'd rather take a sharp stick in the eye.

"I'd go with you and introduce myself," Jill said, "but I have to get home. Although I'm sure Adam has everything under control."

"And I have to pick up Ty and get him home. It's a school night. And I'm your ride," Cabot reminded her.

"That, too."

"Okay, then. I'll see you guys later."

Cabot's expression was filled with fraternal sympathy. "You're a braver man than I am."

Ben laughed and said his goodbyes, then picked up his coffee and dropped his empty dessert plate in the trash before heading in Cam's direction.

There was relief in her eyes when he stopped in front of her. "Hi, Ben."

"Cam." He sipped cold coffee. "How are you?"

"Fine."

He hadn't seen her since yesterday morning when she'd broken up the housekeeping hostilities. "Is there a cease-fire at the lodge?"

"For Crystal and Patty there is." That implied not so much with the rest of the staff. "I paired them with other people. They weren't happy, but I pulled rank."

"I think it was General Colin Powell who said that to be an effective leader, sometimes you have to tick people off."

"I'd just settle for a little respect," she said ruefully.

Ben wondered at the twinge of protectiveness he felt. This big-city girl was more than capable of looking after herself. Rich, beautiful and experienced, according to the press. But there was a look in her eyes, an expression that said she was a little out of her depth.

"So, what are you doing here?" he asked.

"I already told you—making the lodge profitable."

"No, I meant why did you come to the Chamber of Commerce meeting?"

"Oh." She shrugged and what that small movement did to her breasts in that tight-fitting jacket should be illegal. "I thought it couldn't hurt to be here to see other business owners in action. Maybe it would spark marketing ideas in the mountain milieu. Promotion strategies for increasing spring and summer bookings. And get a jump on fall and holiday reservations."

"Throw everything at the wall and see what sticks," he agreed.

"Pretty much." She tossed her half-empty cup in the trash beside the table. "I like Mayor Goodson. She's smart to open up some of the town's property for sale and development."

"Maybe. It's going to be a juggling act, though. Growing, but not so fast that we lose the qualities that make life here special."

"Bigger means more people can enjoy special."

"Not always," he disagreed.

"For the sake of argument… Didn't the mayor say that as far as health care escalation goes, right now a grant for the money to add on to Mercy Medical Clinic is the best she can do? An actual hospital needs enough of a population to support it. Bigger would be better for everyone."

"That's true. As much as I'd like to see it built, going too big too fast makes for a weak foundation that won't support the existing residents. Everything collapses."

She opened her mouth to say something, but before any words came out the lights went off and on. He looked around and noticed there were only a few people left in the room.

"I think they're throwing us out," he said.

"Looks that way." She took a cell phone from the small purse hanging by a handle from her wrist. "I need to call a cab."

"You don't have a car?"

"Not one with four working tires. I had a flat. The good news is I noticed before leaving the lodge parking lot."

That meant she took a cab here. "I'm surprised you went to the trouble of showing up."

"I didn't want to miss the meeting."

Anything and everything possible to get the job done and move on, he thought. He'd moved on, made his mark, and when he did it felt as if something was missing. They said you could find anything in Las Vegas, but that wasn't true for him. Contentment couldn't be bought at a high-end store on the Strip. But clearly Cam had things to do, places to go. Except right now she didn't have the wheels to get there.

She started to press numbers on her phone. To call a cab.

"I'll drive you back to the lodge," he said.

"I can't ask you to do that."

"There was no asking involved. I offered. Seems silly to pay for a ride when we're both going to the same place."

She smiled for the first time and it was like sunshine. "I'd appreciate that very much. Thanks."

"Okay." He pointed to the rear exit. "I'm in the back lot."

They walked side by side through the room and outside. His Mercedes SUV was one of the last cars there. He pressed the button on his keys to unlock the doors and the lights flashed.

"Nice car," she said.

"Thanks. I like it." He opened the passenger door for her.

She hesitated, obviously wondering how to get in without flashing the goods. He was going to hell but couldn't stop the anticipation coiling inside while he waited for her to maneuver up and in with that short skirt.

"Thank goodness for running boards," she said.

Lifting one foot, she stepped on it and took the hand hold just inside, then settled her butt on the seat. She swung her legs in and reached for the seat belt.

Ben hadn't seen much more than everyone at the Chamber of Commerce meeting. Maybe a couple extra inches of bare thigh, but that was it. Disappointment snaked through him along with a growing desire to see what she looked like out of that chic suit clinging to every curve. That wasn't likely and it was the kind of regret a guy would carry for a long time.

"Nicely done, Miss Halliday."

"Thank you, Dr. McKnight."

He shut the door and walked around to the driver's side, then got in and started the car. A few minutes later he parked at the lodge and they walked into the lobby with its big stone fireplace, cushy leather couch and chairs and the reception desk off to one side. When he started for the elevator, he assumed she'd be coming, too. Their rooms were side by side.

"This is where I say good-night."

"You're not going up?" he asked.

"Later. Work to do."

When she shrugged, he felt a stab of desire shoot straight through him. "It's late."

"I know." She smiled and it was a little tattered around the edges. "But thanks to you, I'm back earlier than expected. I appreciate the lift. Good night, Ben."

"Sweet dreams." He watched the unconsciously sensuous sway of her hips and heard the click of her heels as she walked away and knew his dreams would be anything *but* sweet. Then he thought of something. "Cam?"

She turned. "Yes?"

"My father owns an automotive repair shop in town and my sister works there. I'll have her check out your tire."

"That would be great. My Mercedes is in the employee lot, and probably the only car there with a flat tire. Just have her let me know the cost."

"Will do. Don't work too late," he cautioned.

"Okay." She walked into her office behind the registration desk and shut the door.

The two of them couldn't be more different, but that didn't stop Ben from wanting her. It seemed to get more intense every time he saw her and she worked where he lived. She'd spend the night right next door. It was just a damn shame that she wouldn't be in his bed.

* * *

"Hello?"

Cam looked up from the spreadsheet on her computer monitor when the voice from the registration desk outside the office door drifted to her. In a perfect world there would be a front-desk clerk on duty, but her world wasn't perfect. She was getting used to that particular customer tone, a combination of surprise and annoyance that they'd been waiting longer than necessary for someone to check them into the hotel.

"Damn it, Mary Jane—" Cam had been through this too many times not to know the woman had abandoned her post yet again.

She hurried out and plastered a big friendly smile on her face. A man was standing there and did a slight double take.

"Hi, there," she said. "I hope you haven't been waiting too long."

"A few minutes." He was alone, in his early forties, balding and twenty pounds overweight. He didn't look irritated, which was a good thing.

Cam's motto was never give the customer a reason not to come back. "How can I help you?"

"I'd like to check in."

"Of course. What's the name?"

"Stan Overton."

She pulled up the reservations screen on the computer. "Here you are. Three nights?"

"That's right." He wasn't much taller than she. "Would there be a problem extending my stay?"

If only, she thought. "Not at all. We'd be happy to take care of that for you."

"Great." He glanced around the lobby. "I've never been

to Montana before and I might want to hang around longer."

"I'm sure you're going to love it here." She pressed some keys and pulled up his information. "What brings you to Blackwater Lake?"

"A combination of business and pleasure," he said vaguely.

"Did you want to use the same credit card?"

"Yes." He pulled out his wallet and handed it over. "Have you been in town long?"

It felt like forever. But she wondered why he would ask. Was "greenhorn" tattooed on her forehead? "Long enough to appreciate how special it is."

"What's your favorite restaurant?"

"I could be prejudiced, but the best place in town is the five-star restaurant right here at the lodge. The chef is from New York."

The man leaned an elbow on the high desk that separated them. "What do you like to do here? On your day off, I mean?"

"What's a day off?" She hoped he would take the remark in a teasing way, but it wasn't a joke.

"I know what you mean." He laughed. "But what I'm asking is if you only had a short amount of time here, what would you see?"

"The lake is beautiful. I'm told the fishing is good." She printed out a summary of the hotel's daily room rate and policies. "I'll need your signature and if you could initial the places I indicated…"

"Sure thing." He scrawled an indecipherable name. "I did some research on the Net and what I found said there are hiking trails and places to camp. Is there any place you would go? Somewhere not to be missed?"

Now she was starting to get irritated. Was he just

friendly or hitting on her? That was just… Ew. Or maybe he didn't get out much. The worst thing anyone in hospitality could do was to show impatience.

"To be honest, I can't recommend any outdoor activities from personal experience. But we have a variety of brochures and the concierge desk is right across the lobby. Dustin would be happy to help you. One key or two?"

"One."

She put it in a folder and handed over the packet and receipt. "Third floor. The elevators are right around the corner." Forcing a charm into her smile that she didn't feel, she said, "If there's anything the staff can do to make your stay more pleasant, don't hesitate to ask."

"Thanks. It's starting out great." He nodded and walked away.

Cam let out a breath and saw Mary Jane Baxter rush around the corner. She stopped short for a second, then just looked guilty.

"I just left for a minute, Miss Halliday. I didn't think I'd be missed."

"You never do."

"I'm sorry."

That statement should have been followed by something along the lines of it would never happen again. Cam was just about to the point of making sure it didn't. "Mr. Overton just checked in. Would you please finish up the paperwork?"

"Of course."

The woman handled people and paperwork flawlessly—when she was there. The disappearing without a word was a chronic problem and needed to be managed, but not when Cam was this angry.

"Are you going to be here for a while?"

"I—" She nodded.

"Good. I'm going to take a fifteen-minute break."

Cam turned on her heel and headed for the exit and the rear of the property. Breathing deeply of the clean, fresh air, she climbed the wooden stairs up to the second-floor deck. Her serenity spot. She looked down at the green grass and beautiful flowering plants in the fast-growing shadows. It was six o'clock and the sun had disappeared behind the mountains, taking the warmth with it, and that was just as well. She needed to cool off.

Just as the irritation started to dissolve, she heard the sound of footsteps, heavy ones. A man's walk. There was someone behind her.

"You look ready for a knock-down, drag-out with that railing, but I don't recommend it."

Ben. The corners of her mouth turned up, which was a minor miracle. She turned. "And yet again you're trespassing."

"I saw you at the registration desk, but you were gone before I could flag you down."

"So… Stalking?" She lifted one eyebrow.

"More of a house call. Someone to use your words with."

"McKnight in shining armor strikes again."

"You look like someone broke the heel off your favorite shoe. What's up?"

"Same old thing. Personnel insubordination." She leaned an elbow on the railing. "My clerk at the registration desk disappeared again."

"Again?"

"I know employees are entitled to breaks. That's not a problem; someone is assigned to cover the desk for a scheduled break. But with her it's chronic, unscheduled disappearances. Every two hours she's gone without a word. It's flaky and irresponsible. And I might have to let her go."

"That doesn't sound like Mary Jane Baxter."

"You know her?" She should stop being surprised by that.

"From high school. The blessing and curse of a small town." He shrugged. "She was student body president. Smart, efficient. Every two hours?"

"Like clockwork," she confirmed.

He looked thoughtful. "Now that you mention it, I recall that she's hypoglycemic."

"Can you dumb that down for those of us who didn't go to med school?"

"Her blood sugar dips and she needs to eat regularly."

"So it's a recognized medical condition?"

"Yeah."

"I'm not a monster who'd keep her chained to her post until she passes out. I can be fair, but only if I know what the problem is." Cam threw up her hands in exasperation. "Why didn't she say something?"

"Maybe it's famous heiress intimidation syndrome. All the symptoms are there."

"I'm a very nice person," she defended.

"Then try talking to her like one."

Cam thought about it and nodded. "Can't hurt. Thanks for the suggestion."

"You're welcome."

Now that she was calmer, she remembered that he'd planned to flag her down. "Was there something you wanted?"

"Yeah." For just an instant intensity darkened his eyes and then disappeared. "My sister checked out your tires."

"And?"

"They're practically new and she couldn't find any damage. No evidence of puncture, but the cap was missing.

Syd's guess is that someone deliberately let the air out." He frowned. "Probably a prank."

"Is it still considered a prank when a disgruntled employee does it?" Her sigh had an awful lot of defeat in it.

Obviously Ben noticed because he slung an arm across her shoulders. "They'll come around. Give it time."

She leaned into him for a moment, soaking up the comfort he offered. Again he made her feel safe, made her miss her big brother. He'd taken care of her in a way her father never had and she missed him every single day. But Ben wasn't her brother and a hum of awareness vibrated through her that suddenly didn't feel safe at all.

She pulled away from him. "It's been almost three months and things here at the lodge are worse than ever. In my experience, people either don't like me or they pretend to be my friend in order to get something from me."

"Betrayal leaves a mark."

She wasn't going to confirm or deny. "What do I owe your sister?"

"Nothing. She took it to the shop and put air in the tire then brought it back."

"A house call?"

He shrugged. "Call it public relations. If anyone here at the lodge needs a good mechanic, put in a good word."

"Okay. Please give her my thanks and tell her that I appreciate what she did very much." She started toward the stairs. "My break is over."

She didn't want it to be over because being with Ben felt like a sanctuary.

"I'll see you around," he said.

Not really a good idea. He was right about betrayal. The mark it left on her was about not being able to trust anyone. Ever. That wasn't much of a problem here, since everyone fell in the hating her camp. So that made her wonder why the hometown hero was the only one in town being nice to her.

Chapter Four

"I put a patient in exam room one. And I use the term *patient* loosely, if you know what I mean."

Ben looked at the disgusted expression on nurse Ginny's face and was afraid he did know what she meant. It was another single woman faking a sprained ankle or wrist or something else as an excuse to put the moves on him.

"Does she have a casserole?"

Ginny grinned, a sign she was enjoying this way too much. "Yes."

"Okay. Is there a chart?"

"Uh-huh." She handed it over. "The home phone number is highlighted and underlined and asterisked."

He looked at the paperwork inside the manila folder. Cherri Lyn Hoffman. Twenty-five. Worked in accounting at the Blackwater Lake power company. Single. Discomfort in right ankle. "Well, I guess we should see what's wrong with her."

"Or not." Ginny headed down the hall to the break room.

"Aren't you coming with me?"

"You're a big boy. I think you can handle this." She kept walking, then turned into the last room and disappeared.

Ben sighed as he knocked once on the exam room door. "Miss Hoffman?"

"Come in."

He did. In this Victorian house donated to the town and turned into a clinic, the rooms were bigger. There was a sink in the corner and walls filled with charts and posters. One for nutrition, with portions of fruit and vegetables dominating. Another was a skeleton with bones labeled.

The patient was sitting on the paper-covered exam table with her legs dangling. Brown hair fell to her shoulders and teased the tight white T-shirt. Some shiny stuff sparkled on the front of it. A denim skirt the size of a postage stamp hit her just below the curve of her thigh and barely covered her...assets.

He left the door open, then went to the sink to wash his hands. "Hi, Miss Hoffman. I'm Dr. McKnight."

"Please, call me Cherri."

And you can call me Dr. McKnight, he thought, but couldn't say it. "What seems to be the problem?"

"I think I twisted my ankle."

"Let me take a look." He sat on the rolling stool and moved toward her, and the very high heels she was wearing. That was the first clue she was faking. He looked at both legs. "Which one hurts?"

"The left."

He looked in the chart where Ginny had noted that, per the patient, the injury was to the right ankle. "I don't see any swelling or trauma."

Cherri stuck her leg out. "Maybe you can feel something."

He could feel it was a sham without touching her or looking at an X-ray. "Why don't you walk across the room for me?"

"All right."

She slid to the step at the end of the table, then stepped to the floor with an exaggerated wince as her right leg took her weight. Turning toward the doorway, she limped on the right leg. After a pivot she came back and favored the opposite side before stopping at the exam table next to him.

She blinked her big blue eyes. "What do you think, Doctor?"

God, he hated this. Several times a week this happened. He wanted to tell her not to waste his time. This wasn't a game and he wouldn't order needless diagnostic tests or prescribe medication for a nonexistent condition. But he was a professional and couldn't say any of that.

"I don't think it's serious." He kept his tone neutral with an effort. "When it bothers you, take over-the-counter medication for pain. Elevate it and alternate cold and heat."

"Thank you. I'm so relieved it's nothing serious."

It *was* serious, but not in a way she would understand. He stood and headed for the door. "All right, then. Have a good day."

"Wait." She moved quickly to stop him. "Don't I need to see you again? Another appointment? Or something?"

"No. I'm sure you'll be fine."

She lifted a covered casserole dish from the chair next to the door beside her purse. "This is for you. I thought you being a bachelor and a busy doctor that you might like something home-cooked."

"Thank you." He took it but couldn't manage a smile. "Goodbye."

"Are you going to call me? To see how I'm doing?"

"I'm sure you're fine."

Before she could stop him again, he walked out, down the hall to the break room. Once safely inside, he shut the door. There was a refrigerator on the wall beside it and he opened the freezer, then shoved the food in with the five or six others there. The fridge was running out of room.

Ginny was sitting at the oak table having a cup of coffee. "We usually leave that door open."

"I know." If only it had a lock.

"Are you hiding?"

"Damn straight," he said.

"How'd it go with Cherri Lyn?"

"Same as always. Couldn't keep the limp consistent." He leaned back against the counter. "That's actually a good thing, because otherwise it would have been tempting to order unnecessary X-rays just to be sure."

Ginny's blue eyes sparked with mischief. "So, are you going to call her?"

"Of course not. What she did is inherently dishonest. You can never trust someone like that."

Talking about trust made him think of Cam, who clearly had issues with it. As far as he could tell her checkered past was isolated in her rebellious youth. Anyone should get a pass on that. Now she seemed straightforward and sincere. He couldn't picture her faking a medical problem. In fact, he'd seen her do a number on her foot and refuse to let him look it over. He wouldn't mind seeing her any time, for any reason. Or no reason.

He looked at Ginny. "I'm losing my patience."

"From where I'm sitting, patients of the female persuasion are on the rise here at Mercy Medical Clinic."

"You know what I mean." He snapped out the words, then drew in a deep cleansing breath. "Sorry. But I'm really frustrated with this situation. This is a medical facility, not a speed-dating event. I have a professional reputation to maintain."

"You've got a reputation, and being a doctor is only part of it. The other part is bachelor."

"You're enjoying this, aren't you?"

"Yes." She grinned.

"Well, that makes one of us. The thing is, it could be dangerous. What if I blow someone off who really has a medical issue because of all the women who are faking it?"

"They shouldn't have to fake it if you're doing it right."

"Ginny—" he warned.

"All right." She held up her hands in surrender. "This is the thing. It's your own fault."

"Mine?" That hit a nerve. "What did I do?"

"How can I put this delicately?" She thought for several moments. "Tough love time. And I do love you. A doctor who isn't married and doesn't have a girlfriend is fair game for every marriage-minded woman or matchmaking mother within a five-hundred-mile radius of Blackwater Lake."

"God help me." He shook his head. "And there's no immunization?"

"Nope."

"So, you're saying I need a wife?"

"Or steady girlfriend."

"That's just wrong," he said.

"Are you gay?"

"No."

"Confirmed bachelor?" she persisted.

"Not exactly."

"Then, what exactly are you?"

"Just a guy who wants this to stop."

"Then you need to hook up with someone so the women will leave you alone."

"I haven't met anyone to go out with." No one except Cam Halliday and she'd only be around another few months. She was leaving town.

And just like that he realized she would be perfect. It wouldn't exactly be faking it, not if she knew exactly what was going on.

The best part was that no one would get hurt.

Try talking to her like a very nice person. Cam recalled Ben's advice as she waited for the employee in question. When she heard the knock on her office door, she swiveled her chair away from the computer and called out, "Come in."

She hoped Ben was right about this, because so far nothing had worked. Her role model had taught her the scare-the-crap-out-of-employees style of management. Her father had managed family the same way.

The door opened and Mary Jane Baxter took a hesitant step forward. She was a very attractive blonde in her early thirties, with blue eyes and square black glasses. "You wanted to see me, Ms. Halliday?"

"Yes. Thanks for coming, Mary Jane." She folded her hands on her desk. "There's something I'd like to talk to you about."

"All right."

"Please shut the door. And have a seat," she added.

The woman's expression said she was terrified, but she did as instructed and they faced each other across the desk. But Mary Jane's leg was moving nervously and she looked everywhere but at Cam.

What would Ben do to put her at ease? Probably ask a personal question.

"How long have you worked here at Blackwater Lake Lodge?"

"Almost eight months."

"Are you married?"

"Yes."

"Children?"

"Yes." Mary Jane almost smiled. "A girl and a boy."

"That's really nice. Are they in school?"

"When the youngest, my daughter, started first grade, I decided to go back to work."

The woman still looked tense enough to snap in two. What else could she try? Mary Jane was already scared, so maybe it would be effective to do the exact opposite of her father. Take down the barriers.

Cam stood, rounded the desk and sat in the other chair beside her employee. *And stop keeping her in suspense.* "I might as well come to the point. We need to talk about your unscheduled breaks from the registration desk. Because that's the first place our guests see, there really needs to be someone behind it at all times to greet and take care of the customer."

"I know." Mary Jane twisted her fingers together in her lap. "My husband was laid off recently. I really need this job."

"You're good at it. When you're there, your performance is exemplary. Efficient. Friendly. And you have a fantastic way of calming down the most irate customer. My issue is with you disappearing."

"It won't happen again. Really, Ms. Halliday—"

Cam held up a hand. "The thing is, I was talking to Ben McKnight and he mentioned that you need to eat every two hours for health reasons."

"I can't believe he remembers that." Her leg stopped moving. "It's true. I get lightheaded if I don't have something regularly."

"Is there a reason you don't keep snacks at the desk?"

For just a second there was a wry look in her blue eyes. "There's a company rule against it."

"A stupid rule. Fortunately I can do something about that." Cam tapped her lip thoughtfully. "Keep whatever you need in a drawer. Obviously if a customer is there, don't grab a handful of cheese puffs, but you already know that. In a discreet way, do what you need to do to take care of yourself. I can't afford to lose you."

"Really?"

"I wouldn't say it if I didn't mean it." Cam figured she had nothing to lose by putting it all out there. Again, the opposite of Dean Halliday Senior. "This hotel is in financial trouble."

"There were rumors," the other woman admitted.

"I'm here to turn things around. Part of that hinges on employee retention. Training is expensive and time-consuming. If I can't do what I'm supposed to, the property will be closed down or sold. A lot of jobs will be in jeopardy. Maybe I shouldn't say anything, but the situation is serious."

Mary Jane nodded. "Not knowing what's going on is the worst. Thanks for being honest. I appreciate it."

"So, we're okay and on the same page? Just to make it clear, if you need to leave the desk, for any reason, just let me or someone else know to cover you."

"Of course. Thanks, Ms. Halliday—"

"Please call me Cam."

"Okay. Cam. And I'm M.J." She smiled, a genuinely warm look.

It was the first friendly expression she'd seen in Blackwater Lake from anyone other than Ben. This talking like a nice person was working for her. And that made Cam wonder.

"Can I ask you, M.J., why you didn't just come and talk to me about this?"

"I was intimidated. You're the Halliday Hospitality heiress. Famous. And I'm just—me." She pushed her black glasses up more firmly on her nose. "I didn't want to ask for special treatment."

Cam smiled at the fact that Ben was right. "It's not special treatment from my point of view. Frankly, I'd rather have you on your feet than passed out behind the desk. Just be healthy. That's an order."

"Yes, ma'am." She saluted smartly.

Cam laughed. Since a fragile connection had been established, this might be her only chance to find out a little about her McKnight in shining armor. "Ben said he knew you in high school."

M.J. nodded. "And we went to college together. He could have gone out of state anywhere because his grades were scary good. But he didn't."

"Why?"

"Didn't want to leave his girlfriend. Judy Coulter." There was a sharp edge in her voice when she said the name. "For a smart guy, he was really stupid over her."

"Oh?"

"He'd been accepted to medical school in California and proposed to her so they could go together. She turned him down. Said she wasn't ready yet. Six months later she met a ski bum. Arrogant jerk talked about the Olympic team as if he'd made it. Said he was going to be a star and make a fortune in endorsements. She married *him*."

"Ouch." Poor Ben. What kind of idiot would turn her back on a man like him? "Did he take it hard?"

"I heard he nearly flunked out of med school." She shrugged. "But he didn't. And he got the last laugh."

"How's that?"

"The bum didn't make the Olympic team and Ben made a bundle on his medical practice in Las Vegas. He sold it before moving back here." M.J. smiled. "He really dodged a bullet."

"Sounds like it."

Cam couldn't help wondering if he felt that way. There was something about that first love. Not in her case, because no one had ever loved her for herself. It was the Halliday name and wealth that were the draw.

But that was old news. The good thing was she was doing girl talk and employee bonding. It felt good, really good. And she had Ben to thank for it. And she would.

"She moved back to Blackwater Lake a few months ago," M.J. added.

"His old girlfriend is here in town, too?"

The other woman nodded. "I haven't heard that they've seen each other, but it makes you wonder."

Yes, it did. But Cam couldn't afford to get sidetracked by stuff like that.

"I'm really glad we cleared the air, M.J." She stood and started for the door.

"Me, too."

"There's something I think you should know."

"What is it?" Cam met her gaze.

"The guest that you checked in. Mr. Overton. He's been asking the staff a lot of questions."

"Has he been inappropriate with them?" That's the last thing she needed.

M.J. shook her head. "Mostly he's been curious about you and your family."

"Most people are," Cam said. "But we're just people who put their pants on one leg at a time. Like everyone else."

"I just thought you should know. I have to get back."

She smiled at her employee. "Keep up the good work."

"Thanks, Cam."

After dinner in her suite, Cam was too excited to stay put and decided to get some air. She grabbed a sweater and went out in the hall, her gaze drawn to Ben's door. It was tempting to knock, but he was a paying customer and disturbing a guest's privacy was something a Halliday would never do.

She left the lodge by a rear entrance and walked up the back steps to her serenity spot. It was the first time since coming to Blackwater Lake that she'd come here when she didn't need to find her serenity. She was in the best mood and realized it was about possibilities. There were still mountains to climb and hurdles to get over, but those were for another day. This was a time to savor even minuscule progress.

At the top of the stairs, she automatically looked around for Ben. The last two times she'd been up here it was to get her temper under control when she'd had a bad day and he'd helped her do that. Today was a good day and things continued to go her way when she saw him in the same place he'd been the night he startled her.

"Hi," she said.

"Hey." There was no automatic grin or welcoming smile.

"I was hoping I'd see you." She walked closer.

"Oh?"

"Yes." She sat in the Adirondack chair beside his. The spotlight illuminated his expression and it wasn't happy. He looked a little broody. "What's wrong?"

"I'm trespassing. This time I've got a reason. I'm borrowing your serenity. I hope you don't need it tonight."

"I don't, actually. Bad day?" she asked.

"You could say that."

"Want to talk about it?"

He shook his head. "Not when you look like that."

"Like what?"

"Like you're *not* dying to kick the snot out of something." He settled his linked hands over his flat abdomen. "I was hoping I'd see you, too. There's something I'd like to talk to you about."

"What?"

"You first. Tell me why you're smiling from ear to ear."

"I took your advice," she said.

"Good for you. I'm glad it worked out. What advice would that be?"

"I talked to Mary Jane—M.J."

"What happened?"

"You were right. She was disappearing to eat because she couldn't have food at her desk. There's a company rule against doing that, so I made a unilateral decision to change the rule. Now she's going to keep snacks with her. The conversation went really well. You were right about something else, too. She *was* intimidated by me, but I think she's reassured now."

"I'm glad." He didn't sound glad. He sounded crabby.

Maybe she could cheer him up. "It's all because of you that we're okay now. Thanks for the suggestion. I owe you one."

"Funny you should say that." He looked at her and there was a spark in his eyes. "I have a favor to ask you."

"I'm in a really good mood. Ask away."

"I'd like you to be my pretend girlfriend."

Chapter Five

Cam stared at him for several moments. Surely she must ave heard wrong. "Did you just say you want me to be our *pretend* girlfriend?"

"Yes. What do you think?"

It was a good thing she was already sitting down. "I hink I'll pretend you didn't just ask me that."

"Why?" He sat forward, all semblance of relaxation isappearing. Tension rolled off him in waves. "You said was cute. And a good catch because I'm a doctor. Is there omething wrong with me?"

"Not on the outside, but I'm thinking a psych evalua-ion might not be a bad idea."

"That's harsh. It's not like I asked you to run away and et married."

"For reasons I can't even begin to explain, that would e less shocking." She stared at him, waiting for the easy mile. Disturbing though it was, she would even prefer that hot, smoldery look in his eyes that made her a little weak in the knees. She didn't see either, just the frown indicating something was bothering him. "Tell me what's going on. You don't look like yourself, Ben."

"If only that were true."

"Stop being cryptic and—dare I say it?—a little sulky a tad pouty. Tell me what the problem is."

"Okay." He met her gaze. "Women won't leave me alone."

She waited for more explanation or a punch line indicating that he was joking. Neither happened and she couldn't help it. She started laughing. When his expression grew more intense she said, "You can't be serious."

"Why not?"

"Because most men would give anything to have a problem like that."

"I'm not most men." Now he looked downright glum.

"Sorry." She got a grip on her grin and did her best to be as solemn as he was. "I agree that you're not most men."

"Why do you think so?" He gave her a sideways glance a flicker of interest breaking up the gloom.

"For one thing, you're the only man in town who's ever friendly to me."

"What else?"

"Talking to you about my problems actually made me feel better. And you had helpful, commonsense advice that was useful."

"It's not that big a deal." He shrugged it off.

"It is to me. Nothing about my childhood, family or internship for my father was normal, so practical is a new experience."

Dean Halliday Senior didn't understand a pragmatic down-to-earth style of management because he'd never lived in that world. And neither had Cam until arriving in Blackwater Lake, Montana.

Ben rested his elbows on his knees. "Good to know."

"Okay. So. Now that I've boosted your ego to the breaking point, tell me what this is all about. Why is it a problem for you that women won't leave you alone?"

"If I was at The Watering Hole—"

"The what?"

"It's the local bar on Arrowhead Way and Buffalo Boulevard."

"Ah." She nodded. "I don't get out much, what with working all the time. You were saying?"

"If I was sitting at the bar and a woman started a conversation, I'd happily participate. It's public. It's expected. It's honest. It's a way to meet people."

The Fireside restaurant here at the lodge was public. Maybe it was just that all her life she'd endured photographers ambushing her wherever she went, whatever she was doing, because she'd been concerned that his privacy was violated when he'd been eating alone.

"So you didn't mind that strangers walked over while you were having dinner the other night and handed you their phone numbers?"

"No. I was fair game."

"So call one of them to be your pretend girlfriend. Or, and here's a novel suggestion, maybe a real girlfriend."

"Not a good idea."

"None of this is," she pointed out. "Seriously, Ben, this is like a wacky sitcom episode."

"I'm desperate." He looked it. "Women show up at the clinic with phony ankle injuries or holding their wrists. They're not particularly good at faking it and can't remember which limb is injured."

"Wow. What's the world coming to. No pride in lying anymore."

"Go ahead. Kick a guy when he's down." There was a flash of heat in his eyes but it wasn't lust. More like anger. He stood up. "I guess it was unrealistic to think you'd understand and take this seriously."

"Ben, think about it—"

"For what it's worth, walking in the other guy's shoes is good training when you're developing a management style."

When he started to walk away she surged to her feet and put a hand on his arm. "Don't go. Help me understand. Take me for a walk in your shoes. I'll be good." She held up her hand, palm out. "I swear."

He dragged his fingers through his hair. "Every woman in this town has a mother, grandmother, daughter, niece or friend of a friend and knows of someone I should meet."

"They're just looking out for you."

"More like marriage on their minds. It's like I have a duty to pick one. Even my sister is trying to fix me up."

"So let her." Cam wasn't a good candidate for this. She was damaged goods, so wrong for the hometown hero.

"Maybe I'm old-fashioned, but I want to be the one asking for a phone number when I'm ready."

To her it sounded more like he wanted to control the situation and that could have something to do with the high school sweetheart who threw him over for a ski bum. She could see where he'd be cautious, but that was a long time ago. He was too well-adjusted and normal now. Not to mention too smart and sophisticated not to have gotten over it. Maybe he was the stubborn kind who just didn't want to be told what to do, and wanted to make things happen in his own time, his own way.

"I get that. But—"

"Wait. There's more and it's what's really important." His mouth pulled tight. "When someone comes in to the clinic, I'm obligated to help. I've sworn an oath and this ongoing scenario could potentially affect my ability to do no harm."

"How?"

"These women are taking up appointment time, faking an orthopedic problem to get my attention. And they bring food."

"The way to a man's heart—" She saw the warning look and said, "Sorry. Go on."

"The situation is creating an atmosphere of doubt, for me and the staff. If there's any question in my mind, I'm bound by that oath to order diagnostic tests. X-rays. CAT scan. MRI—magnetic resonance imaging. They're expensive and possibly unnecessary. Exposing someone to needless radiation. Also, there's a very real possibility that under these conditions a real medical condition could be missed."

"Sort of like the boy who cried wolf so often, eventually no one listens."

"Exactly." He rested his hands on his hips. "On top of that, it's disrespectful to the clinic, to me and to patients who need my help."

"So say something to them."

He shook his head. "I will if necessary, but it's awkward. Especially if I'm wrong. I'm concerned about my career. You can't understand what it's like to be a doctor, but I know we share a common interest in doing the best job possible."

He had her there. She'd told him about her ambitions and what the stakes were for her. But that brought another question to mind. One she'd sort of asked already.

"Okay, I see your dilemma." She recognized skepticism

in his expression and added, "Really. But why not ask one of the women who gave you a phone number? Why me?"

"Because they all live here in town and you're leaving."

Any flattery she might have felt at being asked just evaporated. *Be still my heart,* she thought. "I'm not sure what difference that makes."

"This is a small town. You can't keep up a pretense for long. The truth would come out and spread like the flu on crack."

"Secrets do have a way of not staying secret. What makes you so sure that would be any different with me?"

"Like I said—you're leaving. We both know that so neither of us would have unrealistic expectations. All the cards on the table. No one gets hurt."

"Okay. All sensible reasons. But here's a thought. When I'm gone, what are you going to do? When the whole thing starts all over again?"

"Good question." He nodded thoughtfully, as if that hadn't crossed his mind. "I could claim you broke my heart. Spread the word that I need space and a very long time to get over you."

"That could just throw kerosene on the fire. Women are nurturing by nature and would be absolutely convinced that they're the one who could take away your pain and rabid to do just that." She met his gaze and shrugged. "Just saying."

"I'm the new guy in town. A novelty. If I'm off the market for a while, maybe this intense interest will die down. An affair would take me off the radar."

Her heartbeat stuttered. "Since when did it become an affair?"

"Bad choice of words. I meant girlfriend."

"Title only?"

"As God is my witness." He blew out a breath. "Basically it will buy me time. If I'm wrong and things get out of hand after you're gone, I'll come up with a plan B."

If she agreed to this screwy dating bargain, the deck was stacked in his favor. He would get everything and she got nothing. Unless they really did have an affair. At least then they would have sex. It had been an awfully long time since she'd had sex. She couldn't speak for him, but a man as handsome as Ben probably hadn't gone without.

"So far this is all about you," she said. They were standing close together and she looked up at him. Way up. "Not to be too selfish, but what's in it for me?"

"Unfettered access to practical solutions to your personnel problems."

"And this is valuable to me—why?"

"Because I know these people. I grew up here. I can help you build a bridge over troubled waters."

"You've already done that out of the goodness of your own heart."

"I could clam up next time you seek out my advice." He shrugged. "A man's gotta do what a man's gotta do."

So he wasn't a true friend. He wanted something from the Halliday Hospitality heiress after all. Just like everyone else. Granted, his motive was more noble than most, and she suspected deep down this was partly about the woman who'd tossed him aside for a jerk. But still he wanted something. Except she'd sort of grown accustomed to talking with him and didn't want to slam the door on that. Another three months without a friendly face was an incredibly lonely proposition.

"You know this is completely nuts."

He looked surprised. "Does that mean you'll do it?"

"It means I'll think about it."

"Thank you."

He pulled her close for what she'd thought would be a

thank-you hug, but it wasn't. He kissed her. His lips were soft, warm, appealing. The touch lasted a shade longer than simple gratitude warranted and then he pulled away just before she melted against him.

"Have dinner with me tomorrow night and give me your answer." His voice sounded a little raspy, a little husky. "What do you say?"

"Okay, I guess."

But she would be crazy to agree to this. Ditto on looking forward to it.

At promptly six-thirty the next night, Ben left his suite at the Blackwater Lake Lodge and walked next door. He knocked and Cam opened up almost immediately, as if she'd been waiting.

"Hi."

"Are you ready?" he asked.

"As I'll ever be." There was a distinct wariness in her voice. Cam looked at his jeans, white shirt and sport coat. "Where are you taking me?"

"Don't make it sound so ominous. There's a nice little place in town called the Grizzly Bear Diner."

"Sounds kind of ominous to me. Am I overdressed?"

"You look beautiful." And that was an understatement.

She took his breath away, which made no sense since she was wearing what she always did to work—a suit. The narrow skirt was lavender with a matching fitted jacket and she had on beige patent high heels. Her makeup was impeccable. There was nothing out of the ordinary in her appearance, so the shift in his awareness level must be coming from him. The more he'd thought about it in the last twenty-four hours, the more he really wanted her to say yes to his idea.

"Okay. Let's do this," he said.

She nodded, but he was pretty sure someone being led to the guillotine would look happier than she did.

They walked to his car in the parking garage and he handed her inside, then walked around to the driver's side and slid in behind the wheel. Ben backed the SUV out of the space and headed for the exit that would take them to downtown Blackwater Lake.

"Is there a reason we're not going to Fireside here at the lodge?" she asked.

He glanced over at her and smiled at her expression. "Yes."

When he didn't elaborate she said, "I'm guessing the food's not better. Best seven-layer chocolate cake in Montana. Just saying."

"It's not fine dining, if that's what you're asking. My criteria for tonight is a locals' favorite because it's always busy."

"I haven't agreed to this insane charade yet."

"I'm aware of that. But I think I can win you over."

"Pretty confident, aren't you?"

"Power of positive thinking." He grinned at her. "Plus, whatever your decision, being seen there together will keep everyone off balance, and that can't hurt."

"By 'everyone' you mean women."

"Men talk, too."

The signal light at the intersection of Main Street and Pine Way changed to green and Ben turned left into the parking lot. The diner was on the corner and the whole block was lined with businesses—Potter's Ice Cream Parlor, Tanya's Treasures, Al's Dry Cleaning. He parked and shut off the ignition, then got out and walked around to open the passenger door. Cam was just sliding out.

"You should know that I always open the door for a lady."

"Even a pretend girlfriend?"

"No exceptions." He thought for a moment and added, "Well, my sister."

"Because she works on cars?"

"No. She's my sister and that would just be weird."

Instead of the expected laugh, her forehead creased in a frown. "I wouldn't know."

"You don't have siblings?"

"Actually, I have a sister. My older brother died when he was nineteen."

"I'm sorry."

"Me, too."

He settled his palm at the small of her back and guided her to the front entrance of the Grizzly Bear Diner. It was Friday night and the place was packed.

They stopped at the podium displaying a sign that said "Please Wait to Be Seated." There was a young woman wearing a green collared shirt with a grizzly bear on the pocket. Her name tag said *Bev* and she was probably somewhere in her twenties. She looked Cam up and down but said nothing to her.

"Party of two?" she asked him.

"Yes."

Bev checked her clipboard. "It'll be about fifteen minutes."

"That's fine."

When he started to give his name Bev interrupted. "I know who you are, Dr. McKnight."

"Okay. This is Camille Halliday."

"I know who she is, too. But I didn't know you knew her. Go figure." But this time she nodded politely and said, "Nice to meet you, Miss Halliday."

"It's Cam." She slid him a glance and said, "Thanks. You, too."

People were waiting behind them, so they moved aside to clear the area. "So what do you think of the place?"

"The decoration clearly incorporates the diner's name and establishes a brand."

Ben glanced at the bear wallpaper, the laminated menus with grizzlies on the front and grizzlies tucked on the side of the greeter's podium. There was even a glass case with plastic bear toys and logo T-shirts and hats.

The bell over the door rang and a middle-aged man with a beer belly walked in. Cam smiled and nodded at him.

"Friend of yours?" he asked her.

"Stan Overton. He's a guest at the hotel. He's never been to Blackwater Lake before and was asking me about the sights."

"What did you tell him?"

"That I haven't been here long enough to see the sights," she said wryly.

"I'm guessing you didn't add that you don't intend to be here long enough."

She smiled up at him. "I kept that to myself."

The bell over the door rang again and Adam Stone walked in with a pretty redhead. He spotted his clinic coworker and smiled. "Hey, Ben." The family practice doctor did a double take when he noticed Ben was with Cam. Clearly he knew who she was. "You've met my fiancée, Jill."

"Nice to see you." Jill had grown up in Blackwater Lake but was younger and their paths hadn't crossed then.

"This is Camille Halliday."

"I didn't know you knew each other." Jill looked from Ben to her and smiled. "So, you're the competition."

Cam shook her hand. "Sorry?"

"I'm sort of in the hospitality business. I rent out the apartment above my house. Adam was my tenant when he first came to town last year. It's how we met." She looked a little self-conscious in the presence of the Halliday Hospitality heiress. "Bad comparison. No way I'd put you out of business."

"I'm relieved to hear that."

Cam flashed a charming smile that would fool the general public but Ben knew better. Jill's rental apartment wasn't really competition, but Cam was concerned about the property's future in a less than robust economy.

"Do you two want to join us?" Adam asked.

Ben met Cam's gaze and shook his head. "Thanks, but we have some things to talk about."

"Another time," Jill said, holding her fiancé's hand. They wanted to be alone, too, but probably not for the same reason.

"Dr. McKnight?" Bev walked over to them with two menus in her hand. "If you'll follow me, I'll show you to your table."

"Thanks." Again he settled his hand on her back. Partly it was being a gentleman, but mostly he just wanted to touch her. He liked touching her and not just her back. A blast of pure yearning poured through him when he thought about touching her everywhere.

The path to their table took them past the counter with swivel stools, then all the way to the back of the diner. He felt Cam's body tighten with tension as people stopped talking to look first at her, then him.

He leaned down and whispered, "Everything will be fine. You gotta have faith in me."

"Words that strike fear in a woman's heart," she said under her breath.

So the lady had trust issues. He could win her over. His plan was foolproof.

She looked relieved when they were finally seated at

a table across from each other. After unrolling her paper napkin from around the silverware, she put it in her lap.

"Smells good in here," she admitted. "I'm hungry."

"Me, too." He looked at her lips, full, defined and incredibly kissable. The lust not only hadn't subsided, it compounded. "I think you'll like—"

"Ben?" A woman passed the table, then backed up a step. "Ben McKnight?"

He recognized the brunette. "Hey, Tanya. How are you?"

"Fine. I heard you were back in town." She looked at Cam, speculation in her green eyes.

"This is Camille Halliday. Tanya Smithson. We went to high school together," he explained.

"Nice to meet you." Cam's eyes were cool as she looked at the other woman.

"I didn't know you knew our Ben," Tanya said.

"We met at the lodge. How's your store doing?" he asked, wondering when he'd become "our Ben."

"Hanging in there. I own the gift store next door. Tanya's Treasures."

"Right," Cam said. "I saw you at the Chamber of Commerce meeting."

"That's why you look familiar." There was a hint of nerves and a suggestion of guilt in her voice. "I didn't know you and Ben were acquainted."

Cam slid him a flirtatious smile. "We've become good friends."

"Really?" She glanced at her watch. "Unfortunately I have to run. Just took a quick break for a bite to eat." She smiled at Cam. "I hope you'll drop by the gift shop and say hello."

"I'll do that." When the woman was out of earshot, Cam's eyes narrowed. "That was quite an about-face. She went out of her way to ignore me at that Chamber of Commerce meeting. She had to walk around me to get to the refreshment table and didn't bother to introduce herself. Whatever happened to courtesy and old-fashioned friendliness?"

"Like I told you. There's the heiress intimidation factor." He grinned. "And you weren't with me."

"If I hadn't seen it with my own eyes, I'd never have believed it."

"What's that?" he asked.

"I've been here for weeks and no one smiled at me. But with you it's like something shifted in the universe. Attitudes altered. You're the cool guy. The hometown hero."

"Stick with me, kid. You'll see that we can really help each other out."

She nodded thoughtfully. "If you can work that kind of magic at the lodge… I mean, change attitudes and rally cooperation just by being my pretend boyfriend, I just might be able to pull off salvaging that property."

"Does that mean what I think it does?"

"Before I give you an answer, you need to know that this isn't a joke to me."

"I never—"

She held up her hand. "My brother was the Hallidays' young prince. He was being groomed from birth to take over running the corporation. When he died, the job fell in my lap and I didn't want it. After that I made choices and they weren't good ones. But now I'm all grown up and it's important to me to step up. For my family. For my brother."

"I understand. And I'm sure you'll do a terrific job."

"Maybe." She folded her hands and set them on the table's paper placemat. "I don't know how to do it right. Dean Junior would have aced being the boss. He'd have made our father proud if he'd lived. I can't do it as well as my brother, but I'll do my best. And if that means winning hearts and minds in Blackwater Lake by pretending to be your girlfriend, then that's what I'll do."

"Let's shake on it." He held his hand out across the table.

She put her fingers into his palm and her eyes widened. Clearly she felt the sparks, too. She was more fascinating every time he talked to her and talking wasn't the only thing on his mind.

He was sick and tired of all the women throwing themselves at him, but this woman could come on to him any time she wanted. He would be very willing to oblige.

Chapter Six

At the Grizzly Bear Diner cash register, Cam stood beside Ben while he paid for dinner. Later she would settle with him for her half of the meal, which had been delicious, and worth being here for more than just the food. She couldn't swear to it, but her impression was that the friendliness quotient from people in the diner had gone up by a lot since she'd walked in beside the handsome doctor. With luck this—*liaison* was the best word she could come up with—would thaw out her stubborn, opinionated employees and convince them to help her save their jobs here in town and get her a better one somewhere else.

After signing the credit card receipt, he took her elbow and ushered her out the door. Spring was on the way, but the air was still cool and she shivered.

"Are you cold?"

"Just for a second." And thanks to him not as much as she'd been since coming here. "The fresh air feels good."

"Would you like to walk a little? I can give you a guided tour of downtown Blackwater Lake."

"I've seen it. But walking sounds good. I'm so full."

They strolled past Potter's Ice Cream Parlor and its brightly lit interior. There were little round tables with chair backs shaped like hearts. Colorful prints of sprinkles, cones and scoops were scattered on the walls. A glass case was filled with different flavors of ice cream.

"So I guess you don't want dessert," Ben said.

"Not even the best seven-layer chocolate cake in Montana." She groaned. "I can't believe I ate the whole Mama Bear burger."

"I can't believe you ordered it." He slid his fingers into the pockets of his jeans. "I have to admit I misjudged you."

"How so?"

"I figured you for a gourmet greens and goat cheese kind of girl. That hearty appetite of yours was a pleasant shocker."

"Why pleasant?"

"Because there will be more dinners and I'm not a fan of eating with someone who takes one bite and pushes the rest of the food around the plate."

Cam liked to eat. She liked good food. But she tried to make sensible choices, not deprive herself. She was glad he favored a normal, not stick-thin type. But what pulled her up short was the mention of more dinners.

As they walked she glanced up at him. "I don't understand. Why do we need to go out to dinner again? We've been spotted. As the cops on all those TV shows say, we've been made."

"And we'll need to build on that—otherwise the plan won't work. It's what a dating couple does."

Cam realized she hadn't thought this through. She'd been so caught up in the power of his aura and how just walking in it gave her Blackwater Lake street cred. That's what had convinced her to agree to the bargain. So far it was working, but she hadn't considered what came after.

"Hm." She caught her heel in a sidewalk crack and stumbled a little. His steadying hand was warm, strong and masculine, and desire knotted in her belly. He was the kind of guy a woman could count on. Heck, the town counted on him. "Our Ben," they'd said. But she wasn't the kind of woman a hometown hero like him made promises to. "Maybe we should figure out exactly how this is going to work."

"We're dating," he said. "Don't tell me a girl like you has never dated before."

"Of course. But it was spontaneous. Not calculated."

She glanced into the big picture window of Tanya's Treasures. Ornate silver picture frames, collectible figurines, crocheted tablecloths and delicate crystal lamps decorated the window. It looked like a charming place. The owner was behind the register counting bills.

"What are we going to *do?*" she asked.

"This isn't rocket science. We'll just do the things a man and woman do when they date."

Her insides quivered at the thought of that. It was the whole sexy gray area of this bargain. Men and women did a lot of very physical things when they dated. But she wasn't going there. Keep this conversation generic.

"I know what people do in New York and Los Angeles. What is there to do here in Montana?"

"Same things. Dinner. Movies. Watching movies at each other's houses."

"We don't have houses," she reminded him.

"You have no imagination," he scoffed. "Your house is right next to mine. It's handy."

That fact was beginning to concern her the most. "But

sneaking back and forth between rooms won't get us seen by the gossip-loving people in town."

"That's true. But it would be fun."

"This is *pretend* dating," she pointed out. "We're not supposed to have fun."

"That's too bad." He grinned. "Because I'm having a great time."

So was Cam. That was the other problem. Too much fun in the past always bit her in the backside. "Let me rephrase. The whole point of pretend dating is to be seen in public doing public things."

At the end of the block instead of crossing the street, by mutual unspoken agreement, they turned and started back toward the diner.

"I think we should hold hands," he said.

Really? Because shaking on their bargain and feeling the heat of his touch sizzle all the way to her toes wasn't enough fun for him?

"No one is watching us," she protested.

"You never know." His voice was solemn, but laced with teasing.

"There's no one around."

"But the night has a thousand eyes."

"That's just creepy. And Blackwater Lake may be many things, but *creepy* isn't an adjective I'd use to describe it."

He laughed and slipped her hand into his, linking their fingers. They were strolling past the gift shop again. "Think of this as good practice. A chance to get used to each other. Make it look more real—"

Cam was just beginning to relax with the touch when she felt him tense. "What's wrong?"

"I can't believe it." He was staring down the street at a woman waiting for the signal light at Main Street and Pine. "Of all people—"

"Who?"

Cam followed his gaze and saw the light turn green. The woman, tall and slender with dark hair, crossed the street. She passed the diner and glanced in the window as she walked.

Ben leaned down and whispered into her ear. "It's time to kick this bargain into high gear."

"What?"

He stopped dead in his tracks, right under a streetlight, and pulled Cam into his arms. "This is another public thing dating people do all the time."

In the next instant his lips were touching hers. Even if her mouth hadn't been otherwise occupied, she wasn't sure forming a protest was possible. His fingers tunneled into her hair as he cupped her face in his palm and brushed his thumb tenderly over her cheek.

His body felt solid and strong and wonderful pressed against hers. Her heart started a weird thumping as he nibbled quick little kisses over her mouth and jaw, inching toward her neck. His breath tickled her ear and raised tingles that raced over her shoulders and down her arms, settling in her belly. A moan built inside her, but the click of a woman's heels on the sidewalk beside them trapped the sound in her throat.

Ben lifted his head and stared at her as he drew in a breath. Deep down she felt a small flicker of satisfaction that she wasn't the only one feeling *something.* It was a really good kiss. Unfortunately it didn't last nearly long enough.

The footsteps stopped. "Ben? Is that you?"

He straightened and looked at the woman. "Judy Coulter?"

His ex-girlfriend. The one M.J. had told her about. Cam stared up at him as the realization hit her that he'd recognized this woman before the kiss and that's why he'd pulled her into his arms.

"Ben McKnight." She smiled up at him. Darn it, she had a beautiful smile. "It's been a long time."

"So you're back in Blackwater Lake?"

"Yeah. And so are you. How long has it been?"

"I'd have to do the math." He laughed.

"You were always good at it." She finally tore her gaze from his and gave Cam a look she was all too familiar with. It said you're the airheaded infamous heiress, the one whose only talent is turning outrageous antics into outrageous stories for the tabloids.

Ben looked between them and slid his arm around Cam's waist, intimately nestling her to his side. "Judy, this is Camille Halliday. She's working at the lodge."

"I know who she is." Unlike at the diner, this woman's attitude didn't warm up. That changed when she looked up at Ben. She was very warm to him. "Now that I see you, it seems like yesterday that we were prom king and queen."

"High school was a lot of years ago," he said.

"We used to date," Judy informed Cam.

And you're the moron who threw him over for a ski bum, Cam thought. It might be a long time ago for Ben, but it was new to her and she wanted to get even on his behalf. She wanted to tell the witch what she could do with this walk down memory lane. She wanted to protect him.

She snuggled against him and gazed adoringly into his eyes, seeing the amusement there. "Ben and I are dating now."

"Really?" Large, dark eyes glittered with dislike until she looked at Ben. "I didn't realize that spoiled heiresses were your type."

When he started to say something, Cam put her hand on his chest to stop him. "I've got this."

"Oh?" Judy gave her a dismissive stare.

"Yeah." Cam gave it back to her. "If you were his type, honey, you wouldn't be his *ex*."

"It's getting late, sweetie," Ben said to her. "We have work tomorrow. See you around, Judy."

They walked away and she knew the ex-girlfriend was watching because it was several moments before she heard the clicking sound of high heels on the sidewalk behind them. Cam was angry and upset, but mostly with herself. She wasn't sure where the inclination to protect him had come from. He was nothing if not a nice guy, and a woman like Judy was a cobra. Still, he was a big boy and didn't need Cam coming to his defense. He'd only kissed her to get his how-do-you-like-me-now? moment.

He'd used her. At least it was for revenge, a cause she could get behind, but being used was never fun. Especially for someone like her, who'd been manipulated and tossed aside too many times to count.

But not again. This time she was using him right back and would get something out of the bargain, too.

After clinic hours on Friday, Ben pulled his SUV into McKnight Automotive and stopped beneath the covered area connecting the office to the work bays with hydraulic lifts. That part of the business was shut down for the day with chains across the opening to keep cars out. It was ghostly quiet since all the employees had gone home. He planned to leave his car for servicing in the morning and get his sister to drop him off at the lodge on her way home.

He opened the heavy glass door and walked into the office. There was a high counter where several computer monitors sat. On the wall was a Peg-Board with hooks to hold customers' keys, numbered to link them with the correct vehicle. To the right there was a lounge with chairs and a TV. A side counter held a coffeemaker and a refrigerator underneath it was stocked with water and soda. A vending machine had candy, chips and nuts. It was a comfortable place to wait while your car was being worked on.

"Hi, guys."

Tom McKnight looked up from his paperwork, and immediately grinned, obviously happy to see him. Syd's expression was guarded, which meant happy to see him, something on her mind.

"Hi, son." His dad turned off his computer and slid off the high stool in front of it. He held out his hand and after grabbing it, he pulled Ben into a quick hug. "Good to see you."

His father had just turned sixty, still a handsome man with brown hair that was liberally sprinkled with silver. There were crinkle lines at the corners of light blue eyes that would always show the shadow of sadness from losing his wife too soon. She'd died from complications of childbirth after Syd was born. As the face of McKnight Automotive, he dressed professionally in a long-sleeved yellow shirt, coordinating striped tie and sharply pressed khakis.

"What can I do for you?" he asked.

"The SUV needs an oil change and tire rotation. Can you do it first thing in the morning if I leave it overnight?"

"Sure. Can you spare it?"

"I'm not on call, so if Syd will give me a lift to the lodge..."

"I'm happy to." She looked up from the computer, clearly having listened to the conversation. "But why can't your main squeeze come and get you?"

Ben met his father's gaze and saw the question reflected there, too. Main squeeze? What was she talking... Oh. Right. Cam. So they'd heard about the diner. He'd forgotten how fast word spread in Blackwater Lake, even though that's what he'd been counting on. Apparently the plan was working even better than he'd hoped.

"Cam has her hands full at work and I don't want to bother her." The first part was true or she wouldn't have agreed to the bargain. As far as bothering her? He hoped that kiss was bothering her as much as it was him. He looked at his sister. "Besides, you go right past the lodge on your way home."

That was also true.

"What makes you think I don't have plans? A date?"

"You told me you were taking a break," he reminded her. "Speaking of that, how's the hand?"

She flexed her fingers. "Good as new. You were right about giving it time."

"Glad to hear that."

"Bev Thompson from the diner was in today." His father gave him the what-the-hell-are-you-doing? look. "I didn't know you were going out with that hotel woman."

Hotel woman? That made Cam sound like a room-by-the-hour girl and Ben felt a quick spurt of anger. "When I lived in Las Vegas it wasn't my habit to run past you every woman I went out with."

"You're not in Vegas anymore." His father loosened his tie. "This is where you grew up."

Ben decided not to debate the point. "Cam is a dedicated businesswoman. Ambitious, conscientious and smart."

Syd's eyes widened a little at his sharp tone. "Looks like you hit a nerve, Dad."

"I didn't think taking her to dinner was breaking news or that you guys needed advance notice. It's my private life."

"In Blackwater Lake nothing stays private," his father said, stating the obvious.

Ben knew that but hadn't been prepared for the part of

the plan where his family would find out. As fast as word got out about them dating, it could get out about them being a phony couple. He had to play this just right. Best to stick with the truth wherever possible.

"Things with Cam and me happened pretty fast."

That was true. He hadn't planned to kiss her, but when Judy appeared out of nowhere it had seemed like an excellent idea. After the fact he wasn't so sure, because the taste of her had made him burn for more.

Tom McKnight looked at him long and hard, then nodded. "You're a grown man and I guess you know what you're doing. But I can't help worrying about you. It's what a father does."

"There's no need, Dad. But I appreciate it."

"Comes with the territory, son."

Ben looked at Syd. "About that ride home…"

"Let me change and I'll be right with you." She headed out of the office toward the employee area.

"Why is Syd taking a break from men?" he asked when his sister was out of earshot.

"Beats me." Tom shrugged. "You'd think in a place that can't keep a secret someone would know. If they do I haven't heard."

"I guess she'll talk when she's ready." Speaking of ready… Ben could barely recall the time before Syd was born when his mother had been with them. To his knowledge, his father had been alone ever since she died. "How are you, Dad? Anyone *you* want to tell me about? Are you seeing anyone?"

"I have friends and some of them are of the female persuasion. But your mother was the only one for me." He smiled, but it didn't fool either of them. Tom McKnight was the kind of man who loved fiercely and only once.

Ben wondered if that was a quality he'd inherited, but

seeing Judy again went a long way toward answering part of that question. He felt absolutely nothing for her and wondered now why it had hurt so much when he'd heard she married someone else.

"Your ride is here and it's leaving." Syd had changed out of her overalls into snug jeans, a camisole top and red blazer. She'd transformed from a scrappy little mechanic into a beautiful, sophisticated woman. They said clothes didn't make the man or woman and that was true as far as character, but the change in his sister was truly amazing.

He slid his arm across her shoulders and resisted the familiar urge to rub his knuckles across the top of her head. There would be hell to pay now if he messed up her hair. "You're a very stylish grease monkey."

"I'm sure there's a compliment in there somewhere, but I'll have to dig it out later." Her eyes twinkled when she looked up at him. "Are you ready to go?"

"Whenever you are. I'll see you tomorrow, Dad."

"Since I'm holding your car hostage, I'll look forward to it." He lifted a hand in a goodbye gesture.

Ben followed his sister to the parking lot and got in the passenger side of her sporty red compact. He moved the seat back for more leg room and noticed how close Syd was to the steering wheel. She was a small woman, like their mother.

She fastened her seat belt and turned on the ignition. Before they reached the exit, the doors automatically locked. "Now I've got you where I want you."

"Should I be afraid?"

"A smart man would be. I want to know what's really going on with you and that woman. Consider yourself lucky that I didn't push this in front of Dad."

"Her name is Camille and we're friends who enjoy each other's company."

"Trying to decide whether or not to take it to the next level?"

"Exactly," he agreed.

"Is she seeing anyone else?"

"No." He hadn't actually thought to ask her that question.

"Are you?"

"No." That he was sure about.

Syd shook her head and tightened her hands on the steering wheel. "I don't buy it. She's not your type."

That's what Judy had said. And how did they figure that? "What *is* my type?"

"Not a hotel heiress who went to the slammer, I can tell you that."

The slammer was a long time ago and everyone was entitled to a second chance. Cam had definitely made the most of hers. "Have you been talking to Judy Coulter?"

"I wouldn't waste my breath on that...witch." She glanced over at him. "Why?"

"Cam and I ran into her."

Syd glanced at him. "You're trying to change the subject, but it won't work."

"What exactly is the subject?"

"Your personal life. I have questions. Starting with: For a guy who's been avoiding a serious relationship for a very long time, you picked the wrong woman to break the dating fast."

"That's not a question, it's a statement," he pointed out.

"The question is implied," she shot back.

"How do you know I haven't dated?"

The question *was* a diversion to get her off the scent. When had his sister become so perceptive? Ben hadn't counted on that either.

"I listen. You should try it sometime." She flashed him

a grin. "The thing is, I tuck away information. And women just know this stuff. There hasn't been anyone serious for you, not since college. Now the first one you pick is the type to get her name in the papers for all the wrong reasons?"

"For the record, I don't have a type."

"And it has to be said, that's all the debate strategy you've got?"

"Yes." The less he said, the better. "No type."

"Baloney. You have one and Cam Halliday isn't it. There's something fishy going on here."

"To quote you, baloney. There's nothing fishy about an attraction to a beautiful, brainy woman with a terrific sense of humor," he defended. And a body that makes a man's palms sweat.

What else could he do? If this ruse was going to work, everyone had to believe they were a couple. When the message spread and sank in, women would back off and leave him alone. He'd get peace and quiet at work. Was that really too much to ask?

"She is pretty," Syd conceded. "And a great dresser. I'd give almost anything to have a shoe wardrobe like hers. But I'll have to reluctantly take your word for the rest."

The rest was a petite package who'd kissed him back. A kiss that packed a punch and he hoped she'd "hit" him with it again. The fact that she turned him on would make it really easy to play the part of her boyfriend.

"It sounds like you're smitten."

"I definitely am," he agreed.

"Then you should bring her to dinner Sunday night. It's family night. We'd all like to get to know her." She pulled the car into the Blackwater Lake Lodge and braked to a stop by the front door.

Ben released his seat belt and tried to think of a way out

of this one. It would be easy to play his part with people who didn't know him, but him and Cam spending time with his family was a recipe for disaster. If he put up a protest the way he wanted to right now, it would be like pouring kerosene on the flames of his sister's curiosity. She was already suspicious and would want to know why he was hiding Cam from them.

He hoped he didn't regret this. "That sounds great. What time and what can we bring?"

"Dad's barbecuing and we'll eat around six. Why don't you bring that seven-layer chocolate cake from the lodge restaurant that everyone in town is raving about?"

"I can tell you from personal experience that it's fantastic. We'll be there at five-thirty."

"Great." Syd smiled with a satisfaction that was unnerving. "We'll see you then. Can't wait."

"Me either. Thanks for the ride."

"Any time, big brother."

Any time little sister had an ulterior motive, was more like it, he thought, watching the taillights on her car move out of sight. He blew out a breath. It was put up or shut up time. He was going to take his fake relationship out for a spin with his father, older brother and baby sister—the three people on the planet who knew him best. If they weren't fooled it was game over.

Now all he had to do was talk Cam into it.

Chapter Seven

Late Sunday afternoon Cam was sitting in the passenger seat of Ben's car and not a particularly happy camper. Even though he'd said something about more dinners, she'd been hoping that no further action would be required from her for this bargain. Was it too much to ask that gossip from the diner sighting of them together would hold everyone for a while? At least long enough for her to get over that kiss?

"Tell me again why I have to meet your family and eat Sunday dinner at your dad's?"

Ben glanced over at her, then settled his gaze back on the road. His dad lived just outside of town, not too far from the lake, and the way was winding. "Red flags will be raised if anyone asks about us and my family hasn't met you. It's what a normal couple would do."

"Is it what you and Judy did?" There was just the tiniest bit of shrew in her tone and that wasn't a particularly good thing. Was it jealousy? Or annoyance that he'd only kissed her to make some kind of statement to his ex-girlfriend?

"Judy and I were just kids." Was it imagination or did his jaw just clench? Did he still have scars from what happened? "Now, a few pointers about the McKnights."

Ah. He didn't want to talk about the ex. Cam wasn't sure what that meant, but was happy to change the subject.

"Anything you can tell me will help," she said.

"Remember, this is just a low-key dinner. All very normal."

"I wouldn't know about normal. Nothing about my life ever was. Especially after my brother died."

He shook his head in sympathy. "As annoying as they can get at times, I can't imagine losing one of my siblings. That must have been hard."

"It was." Her heart caught as an image of Dean Junior's handsome, teasing face flashed into her mind. "But before I'd even dealt with the loss, the burden of responsibility that he was supposed to carry shifted to me. In the blink of an eye I was the oldest child of Dean Halliday. As such, I was expected to take over the reins of Halliday Hospitality Inc. someday." She gripped her hands in her lap. "I rebelled."

"All kids do."

"But I elevated it to an art form. Sneaking out of the house in the middle of the night to party with friends I knew my parents didn't like." She cringed, remembering the chances she'd taken. "That resulted in more than one ultimatum."

"They were worried about you."

"No. They worried that company stock prices would drop. I didn't care about anyone but myself then. All I could see was that the kids I thought were cool wanted to hang out with me."

"Every kid goes through that stage."

"I bet you didn't."

"Sure I did." He glanced over and met her gaze. "To me that all sounds pretty normal."

"Not when the police get involved. There were brushes with the law. Then I was in the wrong place, wrong time, at the wheel without a driver's license and someone in the car had drugs. The judge didn't believe I didn't know. And my last name is Halliday. He decided to make an example of me."

"That was a long time ago."

"Yeah." She looked out the window, at the scenery going by. The trees were green and serene and when he drove around the lake, the sight of sunlight turning the surface of the water to shimmering blue took her breath away. "I grew up and discovered I have a head for business."

She glanced over at him and lost her breath again for a different reason. Ben McKnight was an incredibly good-looking man. He would turn women's heads in Hollywood or New York, cities that had some of the most handsome, sophisticated men in the world. As far as her head was concerned, she was having trouble keeping it on business because of him.

"Cut yourself some slack," he suggested. "You turned your attention to school and proving yourself to the corporation. That means you're focused. And you're going to need to be for the McKnights."

"Now you're scaring me."

"My family has to believe we're a couple or no one else in town will buy the act." He glanced at her. "No pressure."

And if the act was outed, any strides she'd made with the employees at the lodge would disappear. Any career ambitions she'd had would go up in smoke because she would fail the test her father had given her.

She nodded emphatically. "Okay. We're a couple. Got it."

"You should also know that my sister is already suspicious."

"Great."

"We're almost there."

"And the hits just keep on coming," she mumbled.

He turned off the main road into a tract of homes. After following the road around a curve, he stopped the car at the curb of a small house with gray siding and white trim. The tops of the pine trees behind it were visible over the roof. In the front a large expanse of grass was green and manicured. There were three vehicles in the driveway—a small, sporty red compact, a big black truck and a silver Cadillac sedan.

Ben met her gaze. "Here we go."

"I can hardly wait," she muttered.

After exiting the car, he took the boxed seven-layer cake, then put his hand at her waist, guiding her up the drive to the covered porch. Cam could feel the heat of his fingers through her wool blazer and satin blouse. The touch skewered rational thought just when she needed it the most. He knocked on the door and it was opened almost immediately.

A beautiful, brown-eyed brunette stood there. "Hi. Glad you guys could make it."

"Me, too." Ben put his free arm around Cam's shoulders. "Syd, this Camille Halliday. Cam, my sister, Sydney."

"It's nice to meet you." This is the one who was suspicious. Cam smiled and held out her hand. "Thanks for fixing my flat."

"You're welcome." The other woman shook it as she looked over her outfit, including the black silk-blend slacks and Jimmy Choo heels. An expression somewhere between admiration and envy slid over her face. Sydney was wearing jeans tucked into brown calf boots and a long-sleeved yellow T-shirt.

Two men came up behind her. One was a handsome, slightly older version of Ben and the other a good-looking guy who had a strong resemblance to his sons. Both wore jeans, boots and T-shirts. Ben wore essentially the same outfit, which should have been a clue that Cam was severely overdressed. Her heart sank because you didn't win hearts and minds by not fitting in.

She shook hands with both of them. "It's a pleasure."

"All mine," Alex said, smiling. He was a local building contractor. "I can't imagine what a woman like you is doing with my brother."

What gave her away? She hadn't really done anything yet and the jig was up. Then she realized the two men were grinning at each other so she deduced that his comment wasn't about their charade but simple good-natured sibling teasing.

Obviously feeling her tension, Ben tightened the arm he still had around her shoulders. "Don't mind Alex. He's okay when you get to know him."

"Don't keep her out here on the porch, Ben." His father smiled. "Come on in, you two."

"Thank you, Mr. McKnight."

"Call me Tom." He stepped aside as they walked in. "What would you like to drink? Beer? Wine? Soft drink? Iced tea?"

"I'd love a glass of white wine if you've got it."

"Chardonnay?" Sydney asked.

"Perfect."

As they followed the other three McKnights into the kitchen, Ben took her hand. It felt weird and wrong and fake and wonderful. She really liked the strength of his fingers, the warmth and the tingles. The you-and-me-against-the-world touch took a little energy out of her nerves.

Alex pulled a bottle of wine out of the refrigerator and expertly used a foil cutter and corkscrew to open it. Like his brother, he was an extraordinarily good-looking man. Like most women would, Cam glanced at his left ring finger, which was bare. He was probably single and she made a mental note to find out from Ben if Alex was having the same problem with women throwing themselves at him.

"Here you go," Alex said, handing her a glass of wine.

"Thanks." Their fingers brushed and she felt no tingles or anything out of the ordinary. It was a totally different and distinct experience from when she touched Ben and that shouldn't be. The terms of their bargain didn't allow for heat and tingles when touching.

Finally everyone had a drink and Tom said, "Let's go outside."

"Sounds good, Dad." After setting the cake on the counter, Ben slung his arm across her shoulders again, as if they'd been going together for years instead of days.

He was surprisingly good at this pretending thing.

The rear yard was just as beautiful as the front. It felt like a park, with an expanse of grass surrounded by shrubs and flowers. The wooden fence held back a forest of pine trees.

On the covered back porch there were two wrought-iron love seats covered with pads and a couple of matching chairs. Cam and Ben sat side by side, thighs touching and sparks flying. The closeness caused a hitch in her breathing and she sipped her wine to cover it. Alex took one of the single chairs closest to her and Tom sat with his daughter across from them.

"So, Cam, how do you like Blackwater Lake?" Alex

took a drink from his longneck beer. The label read Moose Drool. Ew.

"It's a beautiful place." She glanced at Ben. The twinkle in his eyes told her he knew she was lying. That wasn't fair. The town *was* beautiful; it just wasn't New York or L.A. "We drove past the lake and with the sun shining, the surface looked like glittering diamonds."

Sydney's smile was supposed to look friendly and to her family it probably did. But a woman could see the cynicism around the edges. "Diamonds are a girl's best friend."

"I couldn't agree more." Cam met her gaze. "A girl who doesn't like jewelry is a quart low on estrogen. Call me shallow, but I can't be friends with someone like that."

"Well put," Sydney agreed, grudging respect in her eyes as a smile turned up the corners of her full lips.

"I know my sister is outnumbered by the boys and taking advantage of having another woman around," Alex said. "But please tell me we're not going to discuss the latest feminine hygiene product."

"I think he just challenged us," Cam said. "Sydney, do you want to start or should I get the ball rolling with what's new in shapewear these days?"

That got an actual laugh from the McKnights' lone female. "High five, Cam."

"Well, well..." Alex glanced between the two women. "That sounds a lot like a seal of approval from my little sister, and I agree. Camille, a lady as pretty as you should feel right at home in a place as beautiful as Blackwater Lake."

"Thank you." If he talked like that to all the girls, they'd be lining up to contract his house-building services and a whole lot of things that had nothing to do with construction.

"Hands off, bro. I saw her first." Ben threaded his fingers through hers and settled their linked hands on his muscular thigh.

The resulting wave of heat almost kept her from noticing the slightest edge to his voice and the possessiveness of the gesture. Was this real jealousy, or was he pretending? It was the sort of thing an actual boyfriend might do and felt very real. So real she had to remind herself that this was just make-believe.

Sydney's gaze narrowed as she studied them. "Is anyone else starving? I think it's time to cook the steaks, Dad."

"Okay. I'll fire up the barbecue."

"I'll take care of everything inside." She stood. "Do you want to give me a hand, Cam?"

This was a test, Cam thought. "Of course."

"Me, too," Ben said.

The three of them went into the kitchen where Syd pulled an already-put-together salad from the refrigerator. "Why don't you two set the table?"

"Okay." Ben turned toward the cupboard nearest the natural pine table in the kitchen's eating nook. "I'll show you where everything is, sweetie."

"Thanks."

Was she supposed to add an endearing nickname, too? This phony-girlfriend thing was harder than she'd thought. Play-acting for his family was a lot of pressure, but if they passed this test, fooling the rest of Blackwater Lake should be easier. But the McKnights seemed like a wonderful family. There was a part of her that wished this wasn't an act and normal could be hers.

"So, Cam," Syd said, setting a bowl of potato salad on the table. "Do you like the outdoors?"

Was this a trick question? "I love the fresh air here in the mountains. But work keeps me pretty busy. I don't get out much."

"So you haven't been camping yet?"

"No." That was the truth. Not once ever in her life had she slept without four walls surrounding her that included a bathroom with running water and electricity. She looked at Ben for guidance, but he was just taking plates down from a shelf and the rattling kept him from hearing the question. "Like I said, there hasn't been much time off since I got here."

The look in her brown eyes said Syd was just getting started. "Ben loves backpacking, fishing and camping, don't you, big brother?"

He set the five plates on the table, which was big enough for six people, and put one in front of each chair. "Yeah. I've missed doing that."

"Isn't that one of the reasons you moved back here?" his sister persisted. "Camping, fishing, being outdoors?"

"It is," he agreed.

"Have you ever camped out, Cam?"

She looked at Ben again, unsure how far this pretense should go. It was all a big lie, but lacing everything with some truth would make the ruse easier to pull off. "Since my family owns a hotel chain, the only camping out we did had room service. But it's something I've always wanted to try."

A little truth followed closely by a whopper of a lie.

Ben moved close and settled his arm around her waist. Tension was evident in his body. "As a matter of fact, I'm taking Cam backpacking next weekend, right, sweetie?"

Cam's gaze snapped to his. This was not what she'd signed up for, and definitely not spelled out in their verbal agreement. It did, however, fall into the category of convincing his family. If they were convinced, people in town would be, too.

"Right," she said, shooting him a glare.

Syd pulled a platter of raw steaks from the refrigerator. "Ben, would you take this out to Dad?"

"Yeah." He took it and opened the door. "Be right back."

Then Cam was alone with the suspicious sister. Ben's dad had seemed happy that his son was happy. His brother appeared to approve of her. Sydney McKnight was the lone family holdout and kept staring as if she expected an alien to pop out of Cam's chest.

"There's something fishy going on," she said.

"I guess that happens when camping and fishing are involved." Cam winced at the stupid joke.

The serious expression on Syd's face didn't change. "Just so we're clear, if you break my brother's heart..."

"What if he breaks mine?" That was an automatic response, but for the first time Cam realized it was a possibility.

She liked Ben more every time they were together. That was potentially a problem, because the longer she had to keep up the pretense of being his girlfriend, the more she could see herself falling for him, for real. And now they'd been maneuvered into a weekend trip.

Maybe they could just pretend to go camping.

Cam was standing at the front desk with M.J. and Glen Larson, the general manager. He was tall, dark and nice-looking, in his early twenties and a recent college grad with a brand-spanking-new business degree. The three of them were looking over upcoming bookings. Summer was only a couple months away and she'd feel a lot better if reservations increased.

Shaking her head Cam said, "I have to figure out a way to pitch the positives of Blackwater Lake Lodge to travel professionals and online sites."

"I can help with that," Glen offered. "I've got some experience in web marketing. There's a way to make sure this town and the lodge come up first in the search engine when someone is looking for information on Montana."

"That would be great." She smiled at him, his earnestness and willingness to help. Cooperation was a nice change and there was little doubt that she had Ben McKnight to thank for it. "If you need extra time to work on it, let me know. I can handle some of your management responsibilities. And if necessary and you're okay with it, I can authorize limited overtime."

"Thanks, boss." His surprised tone said he hadn't fully expected teamwork or support from her.

"Okay, now for the employee appreciation dinner next week. We need—"

Her two employees smiled at someone behind her; she'd been concentrating so hard she hadn't heard anyone approach. Then strong hands on her shoulders gently turned her and she saw Ben standing there. Her heart did a little skip and shimmy when he smiled.

"Hey, beautiful." He was looking at her mouth.

"Hi." She blinked up at him, wondering if the glow growing inside her was visible to the naked eye. "It has to be said that there are rules against non-employees being behind this desk."

"Rules were meant to be broken." He took her hand and settled it in the bend of his elbow. "But I respect you and your work so I'll just have to lure you out into the neutral zone and away from all this."

"Good luck with that, Doc." Glen slid his hands into the pockets of his charcoal slacks. "M.J. and I have been trying to get her to go home for an hour."

"He's right. She works too hard. All work and no play..." M.J. lifted one eyebrow to make her point.

"I love what I do and it doesn't feel like work," Cam protested.

"Still—" Ben gently tugged her around the desk to the lobby side. "I've got you now, my pretty. And we have shopping to do."

"Shoes?" she asked hopefully.

"Yes." His eyes twinkled. "Hiking boots."

"What did I ever do to deserve this?"

"She's a wilderness virgin and needs stuff. I'm taking her camping," he explained.

Because his family, specifically his sister, was torturing her. "Lucky me."

"Sounds like fun." M.J. walked into the office behind the desk and returned with Cam's purse and handed it over. "Go. Work will still be here in the morning."

How many mornings after that would it be here if business didn't pick up?

"Okay." She started to turn away, then thought of something. "Wait. One more thing. What's happening with the employee dinner? I know the restaurant chef is handling all the food. Do we know—"

"Today is the deadline for RSVPs," M.J. said. "I'll get the head count to Amanda. I formed a volunteer committee to decorate the conference room. We'll keep it simple. It's being handled. Go. Fly. Be free."

"Thanks." She saluted. "See you guys in the morning."

Ben walked her out the front door to where he'd parked his car, then handed her inside. He went around to the driver's side and got in. "This will be fun. Trust me. Don't look like the Olympic rifle team is going to use your designer shoes for target practice."

"It feels that way."

"You're such a glass-half-empty person. Where's that stiff upper lip?"

"There's not enough Botox or filler on the planet for that when you're talking boondocks and backpacks."

He laughed, which meant one of them was having a good time. Actually, she was, too. Who'd have thought?

Ben drove into town and pulled into the parking lot behind the large sporting-goods store. After getting out of the car, they headed for the rear entrance, where he held the door for her to precede him inside. Straight ahead was a locked glass case displaying rifles, pistols and some lethal-looking hunting knives.

Cam stared at the weapons, then up at her pretend boyfriend. "About that whole execution thing? Are you sure camping isn't like that?"

"You'll be completely safe," he assured her.

She shook her head. "I think we need to renegotiate the terms of this bargain."

Ben glanced around to see if anyone had heard the incriminating statement, then took her elbow and led her to a secluded corner behind a rack of quilted down vests and cargo pants.

"The agreement is perfectly clear," he said calmly. "There's not really anything to define. We're making it up as we go along, but everyone needs to believe you're my girlfriend."

"And two nights of sleeping on the ground is going to convince them?"

"Yes."

"Can't we go to a hotel in a big city far from here and just tell everyone we backpacked into the mountains?"

"You mean lie?"

"We're already doing that," she pointed out. "After the first whopper it gets easier."

"My sister isn't completely buying us as a couple. She knows I like the outdoors and anyone I go out with would have to be willing to try it. And the trying it part has to be convincing. A lie only works if you wrap it in enough of the truth."

"So, I need snake bites, scratches and dirt under my fingernails so she'll believe?"

"Yeah." He shrugged. "Either that or things go back to the way they were."

That meant a return to uncooperative lodge employees and the cold shoulder from the rest of the town. She shuddered. Things had been noticeably better since she'd "been with" Ben. There was an actual *volunteer* committee, for goodness' sake. She was beginning to have a glimmer of hope for upward mobility in her career.

And that was just her. If the deal fell apart, women would start throwing themselves at Ben again. Now there was a thought that she wasn't crazy about. Oddly enough, she liked it a lot less than being able to bring only what she could carry on her back for a whole weekend in the mountains. If she didn't know better, she'd call what she was feeling jealousy. But that wasn't part of the bargain.

"Wow, I think all the fresh air here in Blackwater Lake is beginning to affect my reasoning ability."

He looked amused. "Why?"

"Because I, Camille Halliday, am going to buy camping stuff. The world has gone mad."

He grinned. "Let's do this."

About an hour later, they had backpacks, sleeping bags, a lightweight tent and the sturdiest and chicest hiking boots money could buy. The wiry, gray-haired man at the cash register put the newsmagazine he was reading down on the counter. He must have been the owner, because he was practically quivering with excitement at all the stuff they piled up.

"This be all for you, Doc?" He looked at Ben, then her.

"I think so, Mr. Daly."

"Got your sunscreen and mosquito repellant?"

"Do you have anything that will discourage snakes?" Cam asked.

The owner laughed. "She's a pistol. Got a great sense of humor."

"Yes, she does." Ben put his arm around her shoulders and squeezed.

Cam was getting far too used to that. She liked feeling his strength and that big, warm body close to hers.

"So what's the damage, Mr. Daly?"

The man gave them a very impressive total and Cam started to pull a credit card out.

Ben stopped her and said, "I've got this."

"We'll settle up later." She had skin in this, too, and couldn't let him do that.

He shook his head. "It's settled now."

Unsettled was more like it, Cam thought when her heart started beating erratically. But it was stupid to do that. This was just him playing a part, showing people that he wasn't Mr. Camille Halliday, but a man with deep pockets of pride who paid his own way and hers. Wouldn't it be nice if it weren't an act at all? Talk about make-believe.

The man put the smaller items into bags and slid them across the counter. The newsmagazine caught underneath the plastic bag and fell on the floor at her feet.

"I'll get that." Cam picked up the paper, absently looking at the front as she handed it back. Her hand froze as something caught her attention. She read the headline and her stomach knotted until losing her lunch along with her sense of humor was a real possibility.

There was a picture of Ben kissing her outside the Grizzly Bear Diner and the headline screamed, "Halliday heiress hot for hug-a-licious hunk."

Chapter Eight

Ben wanted to put his fist through a wall when he saw the headline and Cam's stricken look, but she was upset enough for the both of them. He decided to try and keep it light. "Good alliteration."

"I'm so sorry." She glanced at him, then skimmed the article some more. "I was so sure that I was off the rag-sheet radar. This is awful. M.J. even warned me that the guy was asking questions."

"What guy?" Anger curled through him.

"Stan Overton, the sleazy guy we saw at the diner that night. Obviously he was following me and snapped this picture. I was so sure it was all behind me. If I'd thought for a second you'd be involved, I'd never have—"

Ben touched a finger to her lips. Partly because he hated to see her so upset about this trash, but also to keep her from revealing their secret. Mr. Daly was watching intently.

"Let's go put all this stuff in the car," Ben suggested.

She looked at him, then the man, and comprehension flared in her eyes. "Okay."

Together they carried all the bags to his SUV and stowed them in the back. Then he put her in the passenger seat and jogged around to get behind the wheel.

"I'm so sorry, Ben. I should have known better than to get you mixed up in this."

"It was my idea, remember?" He was angry, but not with Cam. It was with the bottom-feeders who victimized someone like her. She'd been through the devastating loss of her brother and hadn't been allowed to act out without every move ending up on the front page. If her family hadn't had money, no one would have cared. "You've got to shake this off. Don't let them get to you."

"I'm not worried about me. Although when my father sees this, and he will, my odds of getting a better assignment at a bigger property are about as good as managing a motel on the moon." She met his gaze. "You need to find someone else to run interference for you."

He didn't want someone else. "Don't be hasty."

"Seriously. Associating with me could jeopardize your credibility at the clinic. I couldn't stand being responsible for that."

"You underestimate the people of Blackwater Lake. They can separate personal from professional."

The outside parking lot lights illuminated the shadow of betrayal in her eyes and Ben badly wanted to make it go away. If they hadn't been sitting in the car, he would have taken her in his arms, so it was probably a good thing they were here.

She shook her head. "This is a lousy situation without recourse. The public believes that someone with monetary resources is fair game for their entertainment. In their minds the question becomes: Is the crown too tight? Are the jewels too heavy?" She sighed. "So I just have to suck it up. If it ruins my life, there's not much I can do. But I won't let them take you down, too. You need to distance yourself from me—"

"No."

She blinked at him. "What?"

"You don't need to protect me. I can take care of myself."

Distance was the last thing he wanted. Taking care of her was the first order of business. This protective instinct was usually reserved for his patients. He channeled it into his profession. With Cam it was personal, more than he'd expected.

"I'm sure you can protect yourself, but dealing with negative tabloid publicity isn't something they taught you in medical school." She wadded up the newsmagazine. "They twist the truth or print outright lies. I'm a demanding diva who cracks the whip. I broke up a perfectly good housekeeping team because they talk too much."

"Yeah," he agreed. "They talk at the top of their lungs."

"That part was conveniently left out because it doesn't sell papers. I've dealt with it all my life. But they'll try to dig up dirt on you, too. It's best if we don't see each other and cancel the camping—"

"Let me stop you right there." He took her hand and the delicacy of her fingers and wrist twisted him up inside. "A backpacking trip is just what the doctor ordered. We'll get away. Let the dust settle. By the time we get back, the whole thing will have blown over."

"That would be running away, and Hallidays don't do that."

"Neither do McKnights."

She was quiet as she studied him, but didn't pull away

when he linked his fingers with hers. "Don't be a martyr, Ben."

"The thought never crossed my mind." He laughed, then turned serious. "Don't let them win, Cam. It's an opportunity. I can show you how beautiful Blackwater Lake is so you can pass it on to guests at the lodge. First-person experience."

"You're saying this is all about business?"

"Exactly." Sort of. Although it was feeling a little more personal than he'd expected.

"Okay, then. Let's go backpacking."

"I must have been high on clean air when I let you talk me into this." Cam walked the uneven trail beside Ben.

There was a slight grade and that took them steadily uphill. Fortunately gym workouts and stair-stepper sessions had kept her in good enough shape so as not to be embarrassed. But at the fitness center you didn't have to carry on your back all the stuff you needed for one night and two days in the mountains. Ben had shown her how to attach her sleeping bag to the lightweight frame.

"You're going to love this," he predicted.

"Wouldn't it be easier to be airlifted in by helicopter?"

"Of course. But there are several problems with that scenario. First and most important, the trees are too thick for a chopper to get through." He looked down at her. "Second, while hiking you get to appreciate the beauty and awesomeness of these spectacular mountains. And—"

"There's more?"

"No pain, no gain. You'll appreciate it a lot more where we're going if it's not easy to get there."

"So it's like banging your head against the wall? Feels good when you stop?"

"Something like that." His gaze was assessing as he

looked her over, checking for fatigue. "Are you sorry yet about insisting on bringing the wine?"

"Never." She shook her head emphatically. "Just because this is the wilderness doesn't mean we have to be uncivilized."

"Unlike the offensive bottom-feeders who write stories for the rag sheets."

"Yeah. Like them." She brushed the back of her hand across the perspiration on her forehead. Wearing a baseball cap, she'd pulled her hair through the opening at the back, getting it off her neck. "That still makes me mad enough to spit."

"Self-control," he warned. "You don't want to dehydrate."

"Gotta love the great outdoors. And, speaking of that, it seems pointless to put myself through this when there's a very good chance that tabloid story will put an end to my career before it even gets started."

Ben handed her one of the refillable water bottles that was strapped to his pack. The plan was to refill them at the stream where they'd set up camp. "I disagree about your downward career trajectory."

"This will not endear me to employees who already think I'm a privileged, ditzy diva. And you don't know my father."

"Then he doesn't know marketing strategy. You're famous. Any publicity will be good for the lodge and the town, too. Local businesses will be grateful for all the customers you bring in and you didn't have to pay for it."

"Not out of pocket, but there's still a price." Self-esteem. Reputation. Dignity. Respect.

"The people who know you won't believe that trash. And everyone else doesn't matter."

"It's easy for you to say that because your life has never

been turned upside down by someone who stalks you with a camera then writes lies about the pictures that are flashed all over the world."

"Speaking of that…" He pulled out his digital pocket camera. "Everyone in town is expecting pictures of us."

She snorted. "We could stage them. Photoshop everything. Paparazzi do it all the time."

"I'm not an underhanded reporter trying to make a buck by slandering a celebrity. And it's the most natural thing in the world for us to take photos on a camping trip. We're supposed to be a couple."

"About that…" She took a drink of water, then looked up, but couldn't see his eyes behind the aviator sunglasses. "I wouldn't blame you if you changed your mind about the bargain. It's not easy being my boyfriend."

"So far it's been pretty stress-free."

"Because we're pretending. What happens because of that picture of you kissing me will be very real. Now you're a target, too. If there's anything to find they'll drag your name through the mud." She handed back the water bottle. "I'd like to apologize in advance for that."

"You have nothing to be sorry for." He hooked the bottle on his backpack. "And don't worry about me. I'm a big boy. I know what I'm getting into."

"No offense, but you really don't. They'll say that you're only with me to kick-start your medical practice in backwoodsville. Or you came back to a small town because you weren't good enough to make it in the big city. Possibly that a love affair gone bad turned you into Grizzly Adams, a recluse who can't hack it anywhere else. They make stuff up. That's what they do and it's the reason I've been single so long."

"Because of unscrupulous reporters?"

"Yeah." She glanced up at him as her boots scraped

across the dirt trail. "They make up front-page lies and the truthful retraction is buried on the second-to-last page days later. But trash sells. Some guys wanted to be with me to get their name in the paper, to get noticed by producers, directors, people who could fast-track a career." She shrugged. "Other guys didn't want anything to do with me because the circus that is my life could spill over into theirs. I've found it's just easier to be on my own."

"Again, I need to remind you that this bargain was my idea."

"Only because you didn't fully understand what dating me would entail."

"There's some truth to that." He nodded. "But we've spelled out the rules and both of us know why we're doing this. I *am* using you for my career—to keep women from turning my medical practice into a farce."

"And I'm using you to rehabilitate my image with everyone in Blackwater Lake. As far as I can see that tabloid story makes us zero for two."

"I think you're wrong." He glanced down. "The goal was to spread the news that I'm not available. One picture is worth a thousand words."

"I hope you still see it that way after you fully experience the fallout from this. Believe me, you're going to be relieved that this relationship is fake."

Cam looked up when he didn't respond to that statement and realized that part of her wanted him to refute what she'd just said. Part of her wanted him to say that so far it had been fun playing out their secret arrangement. But she didn't get that vibe from what she could see of his face.

There was an intensity tightening his jaw and with the stubble darkening it, he looked decidedly uncivilized—in the sexiest possible way. Her heart stuttered and her stomach shimmied in a way that had become unfamiliar, a way she'd put aside because that was easier than giving her heart to a man only to be disappointed yet again. She was attracted to Ben McKnight and it had nothing to do with the agreement they'd made.

Wanting him wasn't part of the bargain, but that didn't stop it from being true.

"Are you warm enough?" Squatting by the campfire, Ben put more kindling and wood on the glowing embers.

"Yes."

The fire was lovely, but Cam was plenty warm admiring how the glow of the sparks highlighted the lean, rugged angles of his face and broad, muscular shoulders. She was warm from the tips of her toes to the top of her head from watching the competent way he'd set up the tent and arranged the sleeping bags inside while she'd gathered rocks and arranged them in a circle for the fire. They'd refilled water bottles, then Ben had fished in the stream, eventually catching the trout that he'd cooked.

"That fish you made was as good as anything I've eaten at the lodge's five-star restaurant."

"Too bad we don't have Montana's best seven-layer chocolate cake for dessert."

He looked over his shoulder and grinned before standing, looking all masculine mountain man. In two steps he was beside her, then lowered all that lean strength to a sitting position next to her, so close that his shoulder brushed hers. Sparks from the friction felt as real as the ones she'd seen when he stirred up the campfire.

"At least there's wine." She sighed and it had nothing to do with the absence of cake and everything to do with the presence of this sexy, competent doctor.

He made her feel safe and she hadn't thought any man could make that happen. They were sitting on a blanket with their backs braced against a fallen log, legs stretched out in front of them, holding plastic wine glasses.

"If I'd known fish was the main course, I'd have brought a nice white instead of Pinot Noir. But when you're roughing it in the godforsaken wilderness, beggars can't be choosers."

"Has anyone ever told you that you have a finely tuned flair for the dramatic?" He shook his head. "We're a couple hours' hike from town, not on an expedition to the wasteland of the North Pole."

"Still..." She finished the wine in her glass and refilled it from the bottle beside her. When she held it out to him, he shook his head.

"What do you think of camping so far?" he asked.

"It's not hideous."

He laughed. "Wow. I'm not sure the Blackwater Lake Chamber of Commerce and Visitor Guide is going to want that as a slogan for their advertising campaign. I can see it now—'Come to Montana. It's not hideous.'"

She laughed, too. "Let me frame that comment better so you'll understand where it came from."

"I can hardly wait to see how you can spin it to rehabilitate that remark."

"It's about me, and I don't mean that in a self-centered way." She took a sip of wine even as the relaxation from the first glass slid through her. "I wasn't sure how I'd hold up just getting here. Would I collapse in a heap on the trail? Break a leg? Snake bite?"

"I can't believe how optimistic you are."

"Seriously. I didn't know if I had the stamina and intestinal fortitude. Heck, I had no idea if I was in good enough shape."

He let his gaze trail over her hiking boots, past the jeans on her legs and long-sleeved T-shirt. His eyes narrowed and filled with naked intensity. "Your shape looks pretty good to me."

Oh, my... Her heartbeat went all weird and thumpy. "Thanks, but I wasn't looking for a compliment, just explaining that I'm happy I made it and proud, too. You know?"

"Yeah."

"I'm more relaxed than I've been in a long time." If the paparazzi could follow her here, then more power to them. She took another sip of wine. "The campsite is cozy. Food was delicious."

"Always is in the fresh air."

"It's so clean and pure. Beautiful here." She dragged in a deep breath, then wiggled to get comfortable. "Although I can't say this log is especially comfy."

"Lean forward." When she obeyed, he put his arm behind her as a cushion, then pulled her against him.

"Much better. Thanks." She automatically curled into him as if she'd been doing it for years, and that was a different kind of danger from navigating the great outdoors. But at this particular moment she was too comfortable and content to worry about danger.

She leaned her head against his shoulder and stared at the sky. The beauty was breathtaking. "I don't think I've ever seen so many stars in my life."

He looked down at her and their mouths were only inches apart. When he spoke his voice was a little deeper, a lot huskier. "That's probably because there's too much nuisance light in L.A. or New York."

"But not here," she said reverently.

"No, not here." He gently put his fingers on her chin and held it at just the right angle for their mouths to meet. Searching her gaze he said, "I'd really like to kiss you."

Me, too, she wanted to say but barely managed to hold back the words. "That isn't part of the bargain."

"It should be." There was a hint of irritated frustration in his voice.

"Why?"

He thought for a moment. "Couples kiss openly all the time."

"PDA."

"Excuse me?"

"Public display of affection," she explained.

"Right."

"The thing is, we did that and ended up on the cover of a nationally syndicated magazine." Funny, she thought, right here and now with a sky full of glitter and the scent of pine surrounding her, the bad stuff just didn't seem to matter as much.

"To convince the skeptics, we need to do it again and make it look good, like it happens all the time in private."

She blinked up at him. "You're saying that we have to practice kissing?"

He nodded. "What do you think?"

That this is trouble, she thought. Trouble she could enthusiastically get behind. "I think if you think practicing is a good idea, then it's probably okay."

"That's not exactly wholehearted agreement." He glanced up at the sky. "Can you think of a better place?"

It was the most romantic spot she'd ever been in her entire life. "No," she whispered. "This is perfect."

"Okay then. Practice makes perfect, too." He shifted his shoulders toward her, getting ready to move in. "This first one we'll need around town. The playful peck on the cheek."

"You name kisses?"

"Don't you?"

It had been so long she couldn't remember. "Not really."

He brushed his thumb over her chin. "Now stop talking and concentrate."

"Okay." She realized she'd spoken and said, "Sorry." She shrugged.

"Here goes." He dipped his head and gave her a quick kiss just in front of her ear.

She felt his breath stir her hair and that raised tingles on her arms. "M-my family does that, but it's an air kiss."

He nodded. "Next up is the haven't-seen-you-all-day. This will come in handy at the lodge if you happen to be at the registration desk when I get back from the clinic."

"Definitely important to practice that one," she agreed, anticipation trickling through her.

"I'm glad you comprehend the full magnitude of the situation." He started to lower his head, then stopped and said, "Keep in mind we'll be standing up for this one."

"Got it."

She closed her eyes and lifted her chin just as his mouth met hers, lips slightly apart. Before she was ready to let go, he pulled back.

His chest was rising and falling quickly. "That was pretty good."

"Thanks." She stared into his eyes and asked breathlessly, "What else have you got?"

He touched his mouth to her cheek and nibbled his way to her neck. "I call that the wait-until-I-get-you-alone."

She didn't have to wait; they were alone.

"Very nice." She swallowed hard. "That's an impressive repertoire. I think that covers just about everything we should need—"

"There's one more we might have to pull off."

She settled her palm on his chest and felt his heart pounding. "Does it have a name?"

"I call it get-a-room."

"Oh, my—"

He called it right, she thought when he touched his mouth to hers. At the same time he pulled her tightly against him and wrapped her in his arms. Heat devoured her when he traced the seam of her lips with his tongue. She opened for him and he willingly took what she offered.

He stroked her and she let him, loving the feeling of being held and stroked. But it was more than that. It was the fact that *this* man was doing the holding making all the difference. She wanted this; she wanted him.

"Oh, Ben, this is so—"

"If you say it's not right, then I'm doing something wrong."

"No. Everything is perfect. Get-a-room delivers in a big way, and—"

He pulled back to look at her and seemed to know what she was thinking. "We don't have a room, but the tent is handy."

It had been so long for her and he felt so good that she just couldn't find the will to say this wasn't a good idea. At this moment it seemed like the best idea she'd ever heard.

"I'll race you."

Ben surged to his feet and pulled her up with him. He tugged her to the dome tent at the edge of the clearing, then led her inside and zipped the entrance closed after them. Cam dropped to the sleeping bag and pulled off her hiking boots. He did the same.

The sound of their rapid breathing filled the tiny space as they yanked at buttons, shirts and jeans. Clothes were gone in what was possibly a land speed record and she was naked in the sleeping bag with an equally naked Ben.

He settled his hand on her breast and brushed his thumb across the peak. The sensation started a throbbing between her legs and she moaned with need. She put her hand on his chest, letting the dusting of hair tickle her palm, and her touch made him groan.

He kissed her over and over until she could hardly draw enough air into her lungs. When he pulled back she nearly whimpered with disappointment.

"What do you call that one?" she asked, cupping his lean cheek in her palm.

"The I-need-you-now." Just enough glow from the fire penetrated the tent to see the primal intensity in his eyes.

She nodded wordlessly and tried to pull him down.

"Hold that thought." He fumbled through the tangle of clothes beside them and finally found his jeans. After pulling something from his wallet, he was back. "Condom."

Cam didn't ask why he'd brought it; she was only grateful that he was prepared. When he'd put it on, he settled on top of her and she wrapped her legs around his waist as he entered her.

He was still for a moment, letting her get used to the feel of him. Then he started to move and in seconds she caught his rhythm, as if this weren't their first time together. He stroked her over and over, then slid an arm beneath her and rolled until she was straddling him.

"What do you call that move?" she asked, gently biting his earlobe.

He sucked in a breath and said, "I've got you right where I want you." His voice was a sexy growl that scraped over her bare skin.

Then he cupped her breasts in his hands and groaned as she arched her hips and lifted them up and down. He reached between their bodies and rubbed his thumb over the bundle of nerve endings between her thighs. Instantly pleasure exploded through her and she collapsed on top of him. He held her until the shudders subsided, then gently rolled her to her back.

He moved inside her once, twice. The third time he groaned and his body went still as he found his release. Cam held him the same way he'd held her. She held him until he relaxed in her arms. It seemed as if they stayed that way for hours but probably was only minutes.

Ben lifted his weight onto his elbows and said, "We better put clothes on. It's going to get cold."

It wasn't the mountain air, but his words and tone that chilled Cam. Holy cow, she thought, sex wasn't even on the list of rules they'd discussed. But now that they'd done the deed, talking was probably mandatory.

When she was dressed and in her sleeping bag, she glanced at Ben. Their shoulders almost touched, but his face was in shadow and she couldn't see his expression.

"Are you awake?" she asked.

"Yeah." His tone somehow said that sleep was the last thing on his mind.

"So that probably wasn't the wisest thing we could have done."

"Fun though," he said.

She smiled in the dark. "It was fun. But this doesn't change anything."

"I know." There was a restless rustling as he shifted in the sleeping bag. "I'm not looking for a relationship."

"Right," she agreed.

"And you're not staying in Blackwater Lake, no matter what happens to the lodge."

"Right again. If it turns around financially, I'm gone. If not—same thing."

"So we're on the same page. Good, that's settled. We should probably get some sleep." He rolled onto his side, away from her. "'Night, Cam."

"Good night."

But there was nothing good about this night, and things *had* changed, no matter what he said. After what they'd done, the reasons for the bargain were less about practicality and logic. Just like that, there was an unforeseen personal investment, at least on her part. Suddenly the "no one gets hurt" clause of the agreement turned into gray area and she had to find a way to shift it back to black and white.

Chapter Nine

Bright and early Monday morning Cam walked out of her suite and came face-to-face with Ben, who was just coming out of his. She hadn't seen him since returning to town exhausted yesterday afternoon. They'd both worked very hard to pretend sex hadn't happened.

"Good morning."

"Hi," she said, brightly, still working to forget.

He fell into step beside her on the way to the elevator at the end of the hall. "Apparently a weekend in the mountains agrees with you."

"Oh? How can you tell?"

"Because you're looking particularly lovely this morning. And relaxed."

That just meant she was a good actress. "Thanks."

If he wasn't simply being charming, that was just proof of how good cosmetics could be. She wanted to say that he was looking particularly good, too, but she preferred the sexy, scruffy, hair sticking up first thing in the morning look. And she'd never have experienced it if they hadn't gone camping. Though their rooms were side by side, there seemed to be an invisible line neither of them was willing to cross here in the civilized world.

A lot of things had changed because she'd gone away with him. For the first time since he'd invaded her serenity spot here in the civilized world she didn't know what to say to him. Finally she came up with, "I miss trout for breakfast."

He grinned. "That's the nicest thing you've ever said to me."

"I was talking about fish. That has nothing to do with you."

"Sure it does." At the end of the corridor he pressed the elevator's down button. "I caught it, cleaned it, cooked it. I feel a deep, personal satisfaction at having introduced you to the great outdoors."

He'd introduced her to more than that, but it was best not to go there. "I'll admit to doubts about hiking into the mountains."

"Doubts? You were looking for an exit strategy until we set up camp."

"You're not going to let up, are you?"

"That's not my current plan, no."

"Okay. I was wrong." Best to keep things light, she decided. "There, I said it."

"You're a big person," he said, looking down at her.

Two dings behind them indicated the elevator had arrived and when the doors opened they got in.

"What's on your agenda for today?" she asked, moving away from him. As much as she liked breathing in the scent of his skin, it was best to keep her distance.

"Patient appointments this morning, then a trek to the hospital for a hip replacement."

"That's close to a hundred miles away, isn't it?"

He nodded. "Plans are moving forward for the Mercy Medical Clinic expansion and part of that is an outpatient surgery center. That will make a huge difference to people here in town."

"And to you."

"Yup." They arrived on the first floor. "What's up for you today?"

"Battle damage assessment."

"Excuse me?" He took her elbow as they rounded the corner to the lodge lobby.

"That article wasn't especially flattering to me and I've been unavailable for the last couple of days since it hit."

"You're welcome for that." He wore a smug expression, but on him it looked good. Better than good.

"Your humility brings a tear to my eye." She shook her head. "Anyway, I need to evaluate the fallout and hope that it hasn't set me back in my quest to win the hearts and minds of the lodge staff."

"I think you'll be pleasantly surprised." He stopped by the corner of the registration desk. "People in Blackwater Lake can be stubborn, but if they decide you're a friend, you'll be one forever. They're incredibly loyal. Don't forget you started to break down the walls and show them the real Camille Halliday, not the one created by the media to sell newspapers and magazines."

"I'm not sure that will be enough." She glanced over to where M.J. talked to the night manager to coordinate any unresolved issues at the change of shift. "It could be back to them calling me Ms. Halliday, or better yet, the rich witch."

"Then maybe it's time for a couple refresher course."

He moved closer and his eyes went dark, the way they had by the campfire just before he took her into the tent. "I call this one the it-will-have-to-hold-you-until-later kiss."

Cam's heart started thumping wildly as he cupped her cheek in his hand, then lowered his mouth to hers. It wasn't a playful peck on the cheek, just a quick touch that left her wanting so much more.

He stared into her eyes and gently brushed his thumb over her jaw. "Have a good day."

This was a really good start. Dangerous, but good. "You, too. Drive carefully."

"Will do." He moved toward the front door and waved at M.J. before walking out.

Cam watched through the floor-to-ceiling windows until he disappeared. Then she took a deep breath and braced for a bad day. After pasting a big, everything's peachy smile on her face, she rounded the high registration desk.

"Hi, M.J."

The blonde looked up from the computer monitor, then pushed her square black glasses more firmly up on her nose. "Hi, Cam. How was your weekend? Did you and Ben have a good time?"

She wasn't getting any unpleasant vibes, at least not yet. "It was my first time. Camping," she added. To distinguish the outdoor experience from her first time with Ben, which had been pretty awesome. "As you can see I survived."

"When they do Survivor: Blackwater Lake, the celebrity season, you'll have to try out." Her smile said she didn't mean that in a bad way. "Seriously, I'd expect nothing less of Ben McKnight. There was no doubt that he'd take good care of you."

"He certainly did." And then some. A blush crept up her neck and she hoped her face didn't look as red from the outside as it felt on the inside. "The mountains are so beautiful. I can't even put it into words. Everything took my breath away."

That was the honest truth in every single aspect.

M.J. smiled. "I'm glad."

"The next time a guest asks me what to do while they're here, I can recommend hiking and camping without hesitation." The other woman looked at her like a proud mother, as if Cam had somehow passed a test. "How was everything here at the lodge while I was gone?"

"No more scum-sucking journalists asking questions, I can tell you that."

"Good to know."

"Otherwise, it was busy. Really busy." She clicked her mouse and pulled up a computer screen. "Remember how sparse the reservations looked the last time you checked?"

"Unfortunately, yes." Cam scrolled through, studying the information. "Is this a mistake?"

"No. The phone's been practically ringing off the hook. The summer is filling up nicely." What looked like teasing stole into M.J.'s blue eyes.

Cam was afraid to trust both the woman's expression and the explosion of business. "This is on the level?"

"I think it's a direct result of the public finally discovering the whereabouts of the notorious Halliday heiress and her hunky boyfriend. Because curious people want to know."

This *was* teasing. A normal give-and-take between friends. And Cam liked it a lot. "You know, I still hate that story, but if it helped put Blackwater Lake Lodge on the map, then I'll gladly take one for the team."

"I didn't believe any of that stuff written about you. The jerk put the worst possible spin on it."

"Thanks for saying so." Cam meant that from the bottom of her heart.

"It's just wrong for someone to invade your privacy like that and imply what he did in that article. Anyone can see by the way you look at Ben McKnight that you've got genuine feelings for the man." She sighed. "Just the way he kisses you goodbye…"

"Oh?"

"Who's kissing?" Jenny the hostile waitress from Fireside walked up and rested her forearms on the high desk in front of them. "Hi, M.J. Hey, Cam."

"Good morning." Her good feeling disappeared and she tensed for the worst. It was best to ignore the kissing question. "What's up?"

"Amanda sent me to ask if you're still having lunch with her today. She said to tell you before you asked that she's too busy cooking to call or come herself."

"That sounds like her." Cam laughed. "Yes, I'm planning on it."

"Good." Jenny hesitated for a second, then said, "She also wants to hear all about your weekend with Dr. McKnight." She shrugged. "And she's not the only one. I'm curious, too. So shoot me. Did you have fun?"

"I had a great time. I'm no longer a wilderness virgin." The two women laughed as she'd hoped. "And the scenery is spectacular."

"A boyfriend like Dr. M doesn't hurt either." Jenny was just stating a fact and seemed genuinely interested.

"That man can definitely hold his own with Mother Nature and enhance any setting." Again that was the truth.

"Amen. Glad you had a good weekend. I have to get back before I get in trouble with the boss." Jenny winked. "I'll let Amanda know about lunch."

"Thanks."

Cam was truly amazed, and the feeling continued for the rest of the day. Dustin from the concierge desk strolled over to find out if she'd had a good time. Then someone from housekeeping stopped by to see how the weekend had gone. She felt as if they'd accepted her, as if she was one of their own.

The good news was that so far they all seemed to be talking to her. The bad was that they really believed she and Ben were a romantic couple. More astonishing was that the staff seemed to be in favor of the relationship, which made Cam feel like a fraud for deceiving everyone.

But worst of all, she couldn't stop thinking about her hunky wilderness guide. Cam wished she could tell Amanda everything and talk this through, but that was impossible. If she let the truth slip to anyone at the lodge, everything could blow up in her face.

Her only other real friend was Ben, and she couldn't discuss him with him? The bargain seemed to be working, but sometimes it was inconvenient when a plan came together.

Ben was glad he hadn't scheduled appointments until later in the morning and had taken his time getting to the clinic. It had been a late night at the hospital when the patient had a complication from surgery. She came through fine, but then there was the long drive home. He'd hung around the lodge longer because of that; at least that's what he'd told himself.

But if he was being completely honest, it was more about hoping to catch a glimpse of Cam. He hadn't. Now he wasn't sure if his bad mood was a reflection of that or simply fatigue. If he had to guess, it would be the former. Yesterday, kissing her goodbye before heading off to work had been the best part of his day.

Camping with her had been such a good time, and not

only because of the sex—although he couldn't deny that was a highlight. But seeing through her eyes the beauty of the mountains, streams and big blue sky he loved and had missed so much had been satisfying in a way he'd never experienced before. She could have been a whining, complaining diva, but that wasn't how it went down. The awe she'd felt was as clear as the blue of her eyes and she'd been a terrific sport.

Seeing her in the morning had been pretty amazing, too. All that tousled blond hair, messed up because he'd run his fingers through it the night before, was flat-out the sexiest thing he'd ever experienced. Even now the memory shot pure lust straight to his groin. Really inconvenient, since he'd just pulled into the clinic parking lot.

His office was on the second floor of the Victorian mansion donated to the town and turned into a medical facility. The first floor had exam rooms and reception and waiting areas. There was a lab for simple tests, nothing sophisticated since there wasn't the equipment or personnel for that. Anything complex went to the hospital. His footsteps sounded on the wooden floor after he walked in the back door and down the hall to the stairway.

After climbing it, he passed the first door, where Adam Stone's office was located. The other doctor was there talking to their nurse, Ginny Irwin.

"So—Bermuda, Tahiti or Fiji?"

Ben stopped and poked his head in. "Are those the only countries in the world without an extradition treaty with the United States? Is there something you want to share?"

Adam grinned. "Very funny. In case you were wondering, we had some patients cancel this morning, so I'm taking a minute to look through these travel brochures." He pointed to the oblong pamphlets spread out across his desk. "Those are the three places I've narrowed down for a honeymoon destination after I marry the love of my life." A satisfied expression settled in his brown eyes. "Jill's going to be one knockout of a June bride."

It was obvious that the man was actually looking forward to committing. Ben could see happiness written all over his face. But tying the knot didn't guarantee a happy-ever-after. His parents were proof of that. When the love of your life dies in childbirth leaving you with three small children and a business to run in order to support the family, it's not especially idyllic. And his father had never gotten over the loss of his wife.

Ben pushed the dark thoughts away. "So, I take it that Jill wants to go somewhere with a beach?"

"I plan to surprise her."

"She hasn't had a lot of good surprises in her life." Ginny looked at Adam with an expression telling him that this honeymoon better be a good one. "If you can pull this off, you're a better man than I thought."

"Wow, that gave me a warm fuzzy. Feel the love." Adam glanced down at the ads for the beaches. "I just want it to be perfect for her. And I want to see my bride in a bikini for a week. I don't think that's too much to ask."

"And there it is." Ben leaned a shoulder against the doorjamb. "Ulterior motive."

"Do you blame me?"

"Absolutely not." He remembered the erotic sight of Cam's naked body silhouetted inside the tent by the fire just outside. Every single cell in his body ached to see her that way again.

"Before Jill's mom died, I promised her I'd look out for her daughter and grandson. She was my best friend since grade school," the nurse explained to Ben, then leaned over to study the brochures. She picked up the one from Tahiti. "So keep this in mind about your bikini-wearing bride. That girl's never been farther from home than Helena." She looked at Adam. "For the greenhorn who needs a geography lesson, that's the capital of Montana."

Ben reminded himself not to get on this woman's bad side. "I think I know where you're going with this."

Ginny grinned. "Take her to whichever one of these places is the farthest from Blackwater Lake. She'd be happy if you pitched a tent in the backyard so long as you're there with her."

"And she's with me. God, I love that woman," Adam said cheerfully.

"Good enough." Ginny patted his shoulder. "Then my work here is done."

"Speaking of work," Ben said, "I'll just go stash my briefcase and get downstairs—"

"Not so fast, buster. The patients can wait a few more minutes." Ginny put her hands on her hips and drilled him with a look. "You were in and out of here so fast yesterday we barely saw you. Let alone get a chance to grill you about your weekend. What happened with Miss Halliday hotel heiress?"

"We hiked up to that stream a couple miles above the lake." He shrugged, hoping to leave it right there. "So, it's time to get to work—"

"And you spent the night?" Ginny asked, not in the least sidetracked or discouraged.

"Yes."

Ben glanced at the other doctor, shooting him a help-a-brother-out look. Adam Stone might be a hyper-observant family practice doctor, but he was a crappy wingman. The grin on his face said he was enjoying this and had no intention of intervening on a brother's behalf.

"How did she handle that? It's hard to picture Miss Four-inch Heels and Short Skirts getting her hands dirty."

"She was a real trouper. Pulled her weight and didn't complain. She actually seemed to take to the whole outdoor experience." Including the kiss practicing and everything that came after. Don't think about it now, he cautioned himself. "She even tried fishing but swore if a miracle happened and she caught anything she'd throw it back. No one was going to accuse her of finding and filleting Nemo."

Ginny smiled. "Sounds like she's got a good sense of humor."

"That she does," he agreed, remembering her insisting on having wine in the wilderness. "I have to admit that I wasn't sure what to expect." He smiled as her words went through his mind. "To quote her: It wasn't hideous."

"So, her not liking that sort of thing would be a deal-breaker for you?" Ginny asked. "If she didn't take to the outdoors you'd be outta there?"

Ben couldn't tell her he had no "there" to be out of. The lying to everyone part of this bargain hadn't really become real until he'd started. With his family and everyone else. He'd been on the receiving end of being strung along and didn't like it. He wasn't that kind of person. In the end, he just told the truth without answering the question asked.

"Spending time in the outdoors is very important to me."

"Not hideous," Adam mused. "I'm hoping for a more enthusiastic reaction when I take Jill to Tahiti."

Ginny clapped her hands together. "And we have a winner."

"Yes." Adam gave her a warning look. "Keep it to yourself."

"I won't breathe a word." She looked at her watch. "The patients will be here for their appointments now. I'll get them in the exam rooms for you. We've got a full day, Doctors."

"Thanks, Ginny. Don't know what we'd do without you," Adam said.

"It's my job." The tone was matter-of-fact, but there was a smile on her face when she walked out the door.

"I guess we better get down there, too," Ben said.

"Just a second." Adam stood and walked around the desk. He was wearing the usual green scrubs and white lab coat. "Can we talk?"

"Sure." But Ben knew those words were never good. "Is something wrong?"

"No." The other man looked thoughtful. "Just something I thought you should know."

"Okay. What's up?"

"I guess you're aware of that article that came out in *The Rumor Report*."

"Yeah. Cam was really upset about it."

Adam nodded. "I can imagine. It was pretty unflattering to her."

"You read it?"

"Someone left it in the waiting room. You were on the cover. Kissing a woman." He shrugged. "I was curious."

"It's not true." Ben folded his arms over his chest.

"So, you're not going out with Camille Halliday?"

Not the way everyone thought, but he couldn't say that. "Yes, we're going out. What I meant was the unflattering stuff that was printed about her. It was blown out of proportion and laid out in a way that would make her look bad. Their goal isn't to tell the truth."

Adam studied him. "You look like you want to punch someone."

"I'm a supportive boyfriend." If you took the "boy" part out that statement was true. He was her friend. "So are we done here? Is that it?"

"Actually, no. I haven't gotten to that part yet."

"Okay. What?"

"Almost every patient I've seen in the last two days has asked about you and Ms. Halliday."

"In what way?"

"They're speculating that you're after her money—"

That had been implied in the article and he had to admit it ticked him off. "I don't need hers. I've got plenty of my own."

"I'm just saying. Don't kill the messenger." Adam held up his hands in a simmer-down gesture. "The other theory is that she's paying you to rehabilitate her bad-girl image."

"No to that, too. Trust me on this. No money is being exchanged."

"I wouldn't care if there was," Adam said. "It makes no difference to me. You're a good doctor and we work well together. I just wanted you to know that the patients you see are probably going to ask."

"I appreciate the warning." And he really did.

Ben wished he could tell his friend the truth, that what he had with Cam was a deal to keep the clinic from becoming a circus because of him. But living with this bargain was different from what he'd expected. People in town obviously had questions about him and Cam. They would be shocked to find out that he had some of his own about the two of them but had no answers. All he knew was that he liked her. Liked her a lot.

Everything was supposed to be casual, but he hadn't taken sex into account. Actually, he'd thought about it almost from the first time he'd seen Cam in the moonlight, but he hadn't thought to include rules about it in the bargain negotiations.

This whole deal had been about getting what each of them wanted. A win/win where no one gets hurt. From where he was standing, it didn't feel like anyone was winning.

Chapter Ten

"Welcome to the first annual Blackwater Lake Lodge employee appreciation dinner."

Cam stood at the head table during the applause that followed her opening remarks and looked around the small conference room. There were about twenty people in attendance, a better turnout than she'd expected.

Actually, since her disastrous track record after arriving, she'd tried to set a low bar for expectations, because the disappointment was easier to bear.

"Did everyone enjoy dinner?" she asked and barely got the words out before the eruption of applause, whistles and woo-hoos. "I'm glad. I'll be sure to pass that on to the chef. And, by the way, everyone who volunteered to serve your coworkers tonight will receive dinner on the house at Fireside. Just a special thanks for your loyalty and spirit of cooperation."

She waited while there was more clapping and a few

whistles. When it died down she continued. "I'll keep this short. I don't want anyone getting indigestion." There was a laugh as she'd hoped. "It's my goal to make the lodge successful and I can't do that alone. Reservations are increasing—"

"Thanks to you getting your name in the paper." The comment came from one of the guys in the back.

"I'm happy to do my part." Cam didn't mind the good-natured teasing. Now that she knew it *was* good-natured. More than one person in Blackwater Lake had told her they'd gotten a glimpse into her world from that tabloid story and seen the ugly side of fame, and she had their sympathy. It was new and different and wonderful. The comment just now had no animosity behind it. "And I just want to thank every one of you for your hard work every day. Without you, there wouldn't be a Blackwater Lake Lodge. Lately I have reason to be cautiously optimistic about the future of this property. If everyone continues pulling together, jobs will be preserved and we may be able to do more hiring soon."

Someone, again probably the guy in the back, started chanting, "Hall-i-day!"

Everyone in the room picked up on it and for a few moments Cam couldn't say anything. And not just because it was too noisy. There was a lump in her throat. She'd never felt accepted anywhere the way she did now. This group had given her a chance, thanks to Ben, but she wanted to believe that she'd won them over because of her fair management style and willingness to work harder than anyone.

Except somewhere along the way she'd started to care about these people, and if the enthusiastic clapping and chanting was any indication, the feeling was mutual. In that moment she realized the effort and hard work she'd put in wasn't just about her career anymore.

"Thanks, everyone." She held up her hands for quiet. "That means more to me than I can put into words. Now I just have one more thing to say. Dessert."

And the crowd went wild as servers brought out the seven-layer chocolate cake.

"How do you think it went?" She sat down and whispered to M.J. on her right.

"Really well. Everyone likes to be appreciated for their efforts and you did that."

"It was short and sweet." Jenny was on her left. She took a bite of her cake. "Speaking of sweet, I never get tired of this."

"It is pretty wonderful," Cam agreed.

"Speaking of wonderful..." M.J. looked around. "Where's Ben tonight?"

That was a good question, but Cam couldn't very well say that she had no legitimate right to have an answer. "He understands that tonight isn't about significant others or a plus-one."

"Somehow he seems like so much more than a plus-one." Jenny sighed dramatically. "Can I be honest with you, boss?"

Cam studied the pretty, heart-shaped face with the dark hair pulled back into a ponytail. There was no hostility in her brown eyes now, just new frankness and authenticity. That was to be encouraged.

And a little levity couldn't hurt. "Should I be afraid?"

Jenny laughed. "A couple months ago maybe, but not now."

"Okay, then. I much prefer candor."

"I'm pretty envious of you. Being with Dr. McKnight. I tried really hard to get him to notice me when he moved back here. And I'm not the only one. Patty and Crystal did, too." She glanced at the two women who were seated to her left.

"I completely understand," Cam told her with absolute sincerity. "And the truth is, I can hardly believe this relationship myself."

"All the single women in town are envious of you. At first no one could understand what he saw in you," Jenny shared. "No offense."

"None taken."

"It's just that he's a great guy and we all had you pegged as a stuck-up, rich, self-centered heiress."

"Don't sugarcoat it, Jen. Tell me how you really feel."

The waitress laughed. "The thing is, you're not at all what we thought. In fact, the unofficial word-of-mouth poll is that the two of you make a great couple. So it's all good."

"That's nice to hear." And the guilt just kept on coming.

"I'm actually glad to see him with someone," M.J. said.

That made Cam curious, and a lot of questions popped into her mind. But it was important to set just the right tone, keep this casual. Too much prying would show insecurity and weakness and make them wonder why she didn't know. Not enough could imply she didn't care and that wasn't the vibe she wanted to project.

"Why are you glad?" she finally asked M.J. Jenny was talking to Crystal and Patty on her other side.

"I guess because Ben came back to Blackwater Lake still single and not in a relationship."

His status hadn't changed, although no one knew, but that still didn't answer Cam's question. "I'm not sure what you mean."

"Me either, to be honest. It's just that I was surprised to find out he'd never been married." She shrugged. "It crossed my mind that what Judy did might have turned him against commitment."

"He's too well-adjusted for that. He's sexy, funny, flirty and gorgeous. And he's a doctor."

"I know. It seems silly to even say it. I'm sure he has his reasons for waiting and that's fine. As long as it's not Judy who's keeping him from being happy."

"I don't think he gives her much thought," Cam said. And she truly believed that. Still, he was the kind of man that most women—not her, but the average female—would give almost anything to be with. "I know he's not gay."

M.J. grinned. "And just how would you know that?"

"I asked. He told me."

"And you believe him?"

"Yes." That and he'd made pretty amazing love to her in the mountains. Memories of that had heat creeping up her neck and into her cheeks. "Any theories about why he's not married?"

M.J. shrugged. "Since we agree he's emotionally stable, one would have to assume he's been busy. After medical school he started a practice in Las Vegas. That probably took a lot of time and dedication. The opposite sex can be a distraction when one is trying to focus on a career."

No kidding. But this conversation was hitting far too close to things she didn't want to get into. Too many questions could imply that she wasn't talking to her boyfriend, which was true. Time to change the subject. "So, how are the kids?"

"Great." A soft expression slid into M.J.'s eyes. "They're looking forward to the end of the school year."

A strategic question here and there had the other woman talking about all the activities available to children during the summer months in Montana. Cam put on an interested face and she truly was. But there was a part of her mind occupied with questions about Ben. Questions she hadn't thought about until M.J. said it out loud.

Why had he never been married? And was their fake romance really about what he'd claimed or something more?

"There's someone here to see you."

M.J. stood in Cam's office doorway smiling a sappy smile. The one every woman wore when she thought romance had come calling.

"Ben's out there, isn't he?"

"Yes—"

"I'm actually in here," he said, moving around M.J.

"I'll just leave you two alone." She walked out and closed the door.

Cam almost told her to leave the thing open. It wasn't like they were going to have sex. Their suites were side by side upstairs and neither had trespassed on the other's territory, although she'd been sorely tempted. But she was waiting for him.

"What are you doing here?" She looked at her watch, which said it was after noon. "No wonder I'm hungry."

"That's why I'm here. To take you out and feed you."

"I have a lot of work. My plan was to grab something quick at my desk and—"

"No."

She looked up and met his gaze. "Excuse me?"

"You're not going to eat at your desk, and I don't care if it's a seven-course meal that takes hours." He came around the desk and gently tugged her to her feet. "I'm taking you away from all this."

"But—"

He touched a finger to her lips, putting a stop to the protest. Her mouth tingled from his touch and she wished he'd kissed her instead. That would have worked really well for her.

"No excuses," he said. "Come with me."

"Where?"

"You'll see."

"Don't you have patients?"

"Not for a couple of hours. There's time." He smiled mysteriously.

"Can I have a hint where we're going?" Passing the registration desk, she waved goodbye to M.J. The sappy smile just got sappier.

His SUV was parked near the front of the lodge and he opened the passenger door for her. She got in and fastened her seat belt, which suddenly seemed an apt metaphor for her life. After he got in the driver's seat, it occurred to her that was another appropriate metaphor for them. He always seemed to be plotting the course. Of course it was working for her professionally. And yes, darn it, she was more personally involved than she'd expected.

"So," he said, "you want a hint about where we're going."

"That would be nice, yes."

"Okay. It's not in town."

"I don't understand." She looked at the smug expression on his face. "We're always in town. That's the point. So everyone can see us together. To keep up the charade."

"M.J. saw us. She'll spread the word that we're inseparable."

For now. But they'd be separating soon. If the upward trend continued, she'd be lobbying her father for a more high-profile position at a Halliday Hospitality Inc. property in a city far away from Blackwater Lake. The thought made her stomach feel empty and that had nothing to do with being hungry. She would miss Ben and that wasn't supposed to happen.

He drove out of town as promised and headed north on Lake View Drive. Trees lined both sides of the road and the sky overhead was big and blue. Big sky country. Words couldn't describe how beautiful this place was. It was something a person had to experience firsthand. Oddly enough, she could feel the tension easing out of her.

"Okay. We're out of town. I need another hint. Is it bigger than a breadbox?"

"Yes. And it has great views." He glanced over, mischief in his eyes.

"Just so you know, I'm not dressed for camping and hiking."

He laughed. "Me either."

The mountain-man look on their weekend trip had been rugged and appealing, but she kind of liked him in the long-sleeved white cotton shirt and khaki pants he was wearing now. In fact, he didn't seem to have an unappealing look. She liked him in anything. Or nothing.

"Are you okay?"

"Dandy." She looked out the window so he couldn't see the heat in her cheeks.

He made a right turn onto a road that went uphill. At the top there was a lot littered with construction materials and in the center there was the shell of a structure going up.

"We're there." He put the car in Park and turned off the ignition.

"Is this your house?" she asked.

"Yes." He reached into the backseat. "I brought water and sandwiches from the diner."

"Good. Because I'm too hungry to wait for you to catch, clean and cook a fish." She opened her door and slid down. "It's like a picnic."

"Watch your step," he warned. "The ground is uneven and there's trash around."

And fresh air. "The breeze up here is wonderful."

He took her elbow in his free hand and guided her over

the uneven ground to where the solid foundation stood and the scent of sawdust tickled her nose. The framing was complete with wooden stairs up to the second floor, but no solid walls separated out the rooms. There was a lot of space.

Ben pretended to open the front door and let her precede him. "This is the entryway and leads all the way to the family room. To the left there will be a formal dining room and the living room is on the right."

"Formal dining?"

He shrugged. "Family dinner on Sunday night."

She walked to the back of the house and looked around. "Is this going to be all windows?"

"Yeah."

"Good. It would be a crime to block a view this spectacular."

"I couldn't agree more." Hands on hips, he stared at the view of the mountains, which was breathtaking. Then he pointed to a spot in the kitchen. "The sink is going there. You can see the lake while doing dishes."

She knew he meant that as a generic "you," not as in *she* would be around to see the lake or do dishes. On the cement floor there was writing that looked like measurements. "Is this going to be an island?"

"Yes. Big enough to land a jet and space for lots of cupboards underneath." He pointed to the corner. "Over there is a large, walk-in pantry. Beside it will be two built-in ovens and a microwave. A cooktop just there and room for a Sub-Zero refrigerator."

"Nice. Really nice. Can I see the upstairs?"

He grinned at her enthusiasm. "Follow me."

She held on to the wooden railing and at the top of the stairs he led her through what would be the double-door entry to the huge master suite, with a large dressing area with his and hers closets. He took her through four more bedrooms, two baths and a big game room.

"How many square feet is this going to be?" she asked.

"Five thousand—give or take."

"Wow." She wandered back to the master bedroom with him behind her.

"Right there," he said indicating a corner, "there's going to be a fireplace."

"Nice." What she wanted to say was *almost as romantic as the stars in the mountains,* but she stopped herself just in time.

He pointed up. "I'm putting in skylights to bring in light for a dreary winter day."

"This is going to be wonderful," she said, filled with a longing she didn't understand. "Who's the builder?"

"My brother. This is the first of a development of custom homes in this area. I bought the lot from him. I'm the guinea pig, I guess. It will be sort of a model for buyers looking in this neighborhood."

"Willing to spend the big bucks," she guessed.

"Alex is looking at a tidy profit margin." He walked over to the wooden window seat, took a napkin out of the bag and brushed it off. "Your table."

"Thanks." She sat and took the club sandwich he held out.

Ben sat next to her with his own. "Bon appétit."

They ate in silence for a few minutes and the breeze drifting around them carried the fragrance of pine and spring wildflowers.

"This is a beautiful spot. And that doesn't even do it justice." She looked at him. "There are a lot of bedrooms in this house. You must be planning to have kids to fill them up."

"I hadn't really thought about it. It's big and that's good for resale."

"So you didn't factor in a wife and children when you had the plans drawn up?"

He shrugged. "Maybe someday."

She studied him, looking for signs of—something. She didn't see shadows or sadness in his expression. "Are you dragging your feet on marriage for any particular reason?"

"Are you psychoanalyzing me?" He chewed a bite of sandwich and there was nothing but amusement in his eyes.

"You can call it that if you want. Or it could come under the heading of making conversation. But pretty much I'm just being nosy."

He laughed. "I don't think I'm a marrying kind of guy—"

She wanted to leave it hanging there, but just couldn't. "Are you avoiding a commitment because of Judy?"

"What do you know about her?" *Now* he looked annoyed.

"She was your high school girlfriend. You gave up a prestigious college in the east to go to school close by because you didn't want to leave her. After graduation you proposed so you could take your wife to med school, but she wasn't ready to leave. You were willing to do the long-distance relationship thing and she agreed. Six months after you left she married a ski bum and moved to New York." She looked at him and shrugged. "People talk."

"Remind me to have a word with M.J." He scowled.

"Did I get it right?"

"Pretty much."

"Does it still bother you?" She watched his expression carefully.

"I hadn't thought about her for years. Not until we ran into her on the street."

The night he'd kissed her. Studying him, she saw no evidence in his expression that he still had feelings for the woman. "Have you had a significant relationship since?"

"I'm feeling a cross-examination vibe," he said, eyes narrowing.

"This is a great house. It would be a wonderful place to raise a family. We're putting on a show for Blackwater Lake, but I feel as if we've gotten to be friends." And lovers, even if it was only one time. Intensity shadowed his eyes and she'd bet he was remembering that night in the tent, too. "I'm trying to figure out why you're building a family house without thinking about a family to fill it."

He shrugged. "I dated in Las Vegas. But I was pretty busy growing my medical practice. There wasn't a lot of time to build a relationship. Women tend to lose interest if they get bumped for a medical emergency too many times." He finished his sandwich and wadded up the paper.

That confirmed what M.J. suspected. "So after Judy you didn't meet anyone who made you want to take a chance on marriage?"

"No. What about you? Anyone special?"

"I thought so once or twice, but they had another agenda. Now it's all about my career."

That was his way of changing the subject, because she'd already told him why she had good reasons not to trust. Once a Halliday, always a Halliday. Her last name would always be well-known and she'd never know whether a man wanted her or the recognition that went with her. But building a career was something she could trust.

"So, I'm curious. Why did you bring me here?" Certainly not for her approval. And he didn't seem like the kind of man who was a show-off.

"This is sort of taking our relationship to the next level."

"I don't understand," she said. "We don't have a relationship."

"Really? You said we were friends."

"Well, yes. But that's a one-level sort of thing. How is this taking it up?"

"My brother, Alex, was wondering if you'd seen this place yet."

"Ah. It would be a logical next step if we were actually dating." She should have known. It was all part of the act.

"Right. So, if you happen to see him, or any other members of my family, you don't have to pretend."

Like she was pretending to care about him. Except it was feeling less and less like pretending.

She'd never met a man who had the capacity to care as much as Ben did. She liked him a lot. She found herself wanting what they had to be more. And now she'd seen where he planned to live. It was a wonderful place to raise a family and the idea of that started a yearning deep inside her for the family she'd always wanted and stopped believing she'd ever have.

She couldn't help thinking what a waste it was that a family wasn't in his plans. That was silly, really, because it wasn't her plan either. But this bargain had become way more complicated than she'd expected and she was beginning to regret making it.

The only thing she regretted more was that she wouldn't be around to see Ben's house finished.

Chapter Eleven

Ben was beginning to regret the bargain he'd made with Cam Halliday.

After seeing his last patient of the day at the clinic, he drove back out to his house under construction. He walked through the opening where the front door would eventually be and swore he could still smell the fragrance of her perfume. In the big open room where the cement foundation was marked off for the kitchen island and cupboards, he could still see her looking out at the mountains, fascinated by the majestic sight. She'd picked up on the fact that it would be criminal to put in any walls and obstruct that view.

He climbed up the crude staircase and remembered the sensuous sway of her hips as she'd moved to the second floor. It had taken every ounce of his willpower to keep from scooping her into his arms and sweeping her the rest of the way up. Unfortunately that romantic gesture would have been wasted since there was no big fluffy bed to put her on.

Then again, maybe that wasn't such a bad thing. It was the only reason he hadn't kissed the daylights out of her before loving the daylights out of her. He'd badly wanted to.

He wanted her so much it hurt.

In the master bedroom he stared at the window seat where they'd sat and the empty bag from lunch. It wasn't littering. Not really. This was his house. Eventually he would move in here. Alone.

Ben remembered Cam's words and the wistful look on her face when she'd said this would be a good place to raise a family. He could picture her here, putting her touch on everything, infusing her classiness into the decorating, adding a lot of color to the landscaping. And that gave him a bad feeling.

Inserting her personality into his life wasn't supposed to be part of this bargain.

It was so quiet out here he heard the sound of a car coming up the hill, then pull onto his lot. In one of the unfinished front bedrooms he looked out the window and saw his brother's black truck. Alex was just getting out.

"Thank God." He needed a distraction. Anything to keep him from thinking about Cam.

Ben jogged downstairs to the kitchen. His brother was carefully looking over the framing and whatever else a building contractor inspected. Alex was really good at what he did. He'd started McKnight Construction in California, then opened a branch here in Blackwater Lake when he brought his pregnant wife here to live. But she'd had secrets and Alex's family had unraveled. Ben wasn't sure his brother would ever get over that.

"Hi," he said.

Alex dragged his gaze away from the heavy-duty metal

floor brackets that held the weight-bearing beams in place. "Hey, little brother. What do you think of the place so far?"

"I think that everything you talked me into is perfect. So far."

"Good." He settled his hands on lean hips. "Like what?"

"The walk-in pantry." Cam's eyes had glowed with approval.

"What else?"

"The window seat in the master bedroom." Ben could still see her brushing her hand over it as if she was deciding on fabric for the cushion. With an effort he pulled his thoughts back to the here and now.

It was amazing how Alex managed to look confident and professional in jeans, boots, T-shirt and baseball hat sporting the McKnight Construction logo. But he carried it off beautifully. "And?"

"What?"

"Isn't there something else I was right about?"

His brother had suggested the corner fireplace in the master bedroom. Ben had pictured himself in a big, fluffy, king-size bed with a fire going and Cam in his arms after making love. It was romantic crap with zero chance of happening.

"I'm not feeding your Montana-size ego anymore."

Alex's eyes narrowed on him. "Bad day at the clinic?"

"No." Work wasn't the problem. Lunch had unsettled him.

"Has Cam seen the house?"

"Why would you ask that?" Ben demanded.

"Gosh, I don't know. Maybe because the two of you are always together." Alex shrugged. "Just seems to me you'd want her opinion on this place."

"I'm building it for me."

Could have been the words or the tone, but something

about that statement had his brother's eyes narrowing. "Is everything all right with the two of you?"

"Of course." Ben's voice was sharper and more defensive than he'd intended.

"That doesn't sound good at all." Alex moved closer, studying him. "Want to talk about it?"

"There's nothing to say."

"You're not a very good liar, little brother."

"What makes you think I'm not telling the truth? That there's nothing wrong?"

"Because you look like someone cut the ears off your favorite stethoscope. What's her name?"

"What makes you think it's a her?"

"Come on, Ben. Tell me what's going on."

"I could. But then I'd have to kill you." He was going for humor, but his brother's expression didn't lighten up.

"Seriously?" Alex shook his head. "This is me. No way I'm going down."

Ben figured he was probably right about that. The guy worked with his hands, swung tools, carried heavy building materials and was in really good shape. Ben ran and lifted weights, but that wouldn't tip the scales in his favor during a physical confrontation with his older brother.

"I was kidding. Just drop it, okay?"

Alex shook his head. "Not when you look like that. Spill it, bro."

Ben wondered when he'd become so easy to read. He really needed to talk to someone, because this bargain was dishonest and so not like him. Realistically, he didn't have much to lose if word got out about it. Cam would be leaving soon and he didn't have a plan B for when she was gone. So what if he confided in Alex, who then spilled the beans? It would be a relief to tell the truth. Maybe when word spread, and it would, women would get the message that he wanted to be left alone.

He took a deep breath, then said, "Cam and I aren't really dating."

Alex stared at him for several moments. "That's funny, because the two of you have been spotted all over town together. And there was that backpacking trip. Your rooms at the lodge are right next door to each other, which makes things pretty convenient."

More like pretty tempting. Ben spent a lot of sleepless nights thinking about her on the other side of the wall. There was nothing convenient about it.

"All the dinners and hanging out? It's not real."

"It looked real. And what about that camping trip three or four weeks ago? Did you, or did you not, take her into the mountains?" Alex asked.

"I did. Just to further the pretense." Sex hadn't been a part of the charade. It had been real, and awesome. Unfortunately, having her had twisted everything up. "This whole dating thing is staged."

"Doesn't look that way. People all over town have betting pools going."

"Betting on what?" Ben demanded.

"When you're going to pop the question. Wedding dates. All kinds of stuff."

"People all over town need to get a life," Ben said. "I'm telling you it's all an act."

"I can't speak for the lady because I don't know her that well. But you're not that good an actor, bro. No offense."

"Cam and I made a bargain. My idea." He didn't want anyone to get the wrong impression about Cam. She wasn't dishonest, just the opposite. And funny, sweet, vulnerable, beautiful. Damn it. Even in his own head he was sticking up for her. "I talked her into pretending to be my girlfriend so everyone would think I was off the dating market."

"The brilliance of that bachelor strategy makes me proud to be your brother." Alex shook his head with amazement. "But how did you get her to go along with it?"

"She was having trouble with the staff at the lodge. I gave her practical advice on how to handle different situations. Because I know most of the key players." He shrugged. "Women left me alone at the clinic. And everything at the lodge is running more efficiently."

"I see." His brother walked over to the doorway and leaned a shoulder against the exposed wood. "So you don't have romantic feelings for her?"

"No." Unless that included sleeping with her that one time. He wasn't sure where romantic feelings fit into wanting to sleep with her again. And just plain wanting to be with her.

"You're just friends," Alex persisted.

"Yeah." Ben knew this man. These weren't just idle questions. Something was on his mind and it wasn't good. "You could say that. Why?"

"Just wondering. I guess you wouldn't mind if I asked her out, then."

An image of Cam with his brother flashed through Ben's mind and white-hot anger roared in his head. No way, he thought. He didn't care if Alex could take him.

He moved a step closer and his hands curled into fists. "Don't go there, Alex. You stay away from her. I'm warning you—"

"Gotcha." The other man grinned. "You're too easy."

It took a couple seconds for anger to fade and reality to sink in. He'd been had, set up. Alex was right. He was easy. "I should pop you one for that."

"Gotta watch those surgeon's hands. Besides, you could

make more work for yourself. On the off chance you did me some damage, you'd just have to patch me up. I'm sorry about that." His brother didn't look sorry at all. "I thought you were feeling more than friendly toward the pretty lady and you just proved my point. I did it because someone had to make you see the truth."

Ben stared at his brother as thoughts raced through his mind, his conversation with Cam earlier. She'd asked about Judy, whether or not he was avoiding commitment because of her, and he hadn't lied. He'd been the one to leave and Judy had refused to go with him. Obviously she hadn't loved him, so he'd dodged a bullet. Eventually he'd realized that a long-distance relationship probably wouldn't have worked either.

His feelings for Cam were threatening to spill over the friendship limitation he'd put on them. And *she* was leaving. He'd suggested this bargain, but she'd agreed because she wanted to go somewhere else. He'd made a deliberate career choice to come back. And no one was supposed to get hurt.

Things were not going as originally planned.

Now Alex had just punked him by bluffing about asking Cam out. He'd done it to make a point. Ben asked, "What truth are you trying to make me see?"

"You've got to nip those feelings in the bud, Bud." Alex nodded emphatically. "If you don't, you're going to be in a lot of trouble."

Ben blew out a long breath. "Tell me something I don't know."

"I really feel awful," Cam said into the phone. Normally she was at work by now, but she was moving slowly. She leaned against the counter in her small kitchen. "I just wanted you to know that I'm going to be a little late today."

"What's wrong?" M.J. asked.

"Same as the last couple days. I'm nauseous and tired. I'll work here in my suite until I can shake it off. Then I'll come down to the office in a while."

"Cam, I'm coming up there," M.J. said.

"That's so nice of you, but really not necessary." She walked out into the living room because the smell of freshly brewed coffee turned her stomach. "It will pass soon."

"That's what you said yesterday. And the day before that. And the day before that."

"I'm okay. Room service is bringing ginger ale and crackers."

"Oh, my—"

Cam couldn't see M.J.'s face, but the tone of voice didn't sound good. "What's wrong?"

"I'll be right there. Glen's going to man the desk for me. Sit tight." There was a click on the line indicating she'd hung up.

Cam sat on the overstuffed sofa and leaned back, closing her eyes. If she could stay like this and not move, everything would be just fine. It was when she sat up or walked around that her stomach turned on her.

She thought about mentioning it to Ben but decided against that. She hadn't seen him for a few days, since he'd taken her to the construction site for his house. On the drive back to Blackwater Lake he'd given off a weird vibe. Probably she shouldn't have asked about Judy, but she couldn't help herself. It would be too sad if that's what was keeping him from being happy. He'd denied it and she believed him, but there was something standing in his way.

Her life hadn't been anywhere close to normal, but even she wondered about building a house big enough for a family when he didn't seem to want one. He might have thought her questions were a hint, that she was trying to change the rules of their agreement on him. She wouldn't do that, but it had gotten her thinking.

There was a knock on her door, which was either room service or M.J. She could take on one or the other but not both at the same time. She managed to stand, walk to the door and open it, all the while keeping her rebellious stomach under control.

Peg Simmons wheeled in the room service cart. She was in her fifties and had more energy than a lot of people twenty years younger. Silver was liberally streaked in her short, dark hair and her brown eyes were warm. And concerned.

"Here you go, Cam." She looked uneasy. "You might want to try and get in some protein. I can go back downstairs and have them fix you an egg and toast—"

"No." She pressed a hand to her stomach. Just the thought of it was unpleasant. "Thanks, but this will be fine—"

M.J. appeared in the doorway. "How's our girl?"

If Cam had felt better the words would have produced a warm glow, but the nausea had put that reflex out of commission along with the rest of her.

She looked from one woman to the other, so grateful that they were on her side now. "I'll be fine," she told them.

"She's not eating," Peg said to the other woman. "Ginger ale and crackers isn't a well-balanced breakfast and this is the fourth morning in a row you've ordered this."

"Have you talked to Ben about not feeling well?" M.J. asked. There was edginess on her face, but something else, too, as she exchanged a look with Peg. It was as if the two of them knew a secret that she didn't have a clue about.

"As you both are aware, Ben is an orthopedic specialist. Nausea isn't in his field of expertise."

"Then maybe you should see Adam Stone. He's a *family* practice doctor." Peg nodded emphatically.

"I don't think it's necessary—"

"Peg is right." M.J. exchanged another knowing glance with the other woman. "Just get a checkup. You've been under a lot of stress lately."

"That's true." She chewed on the inside of her cheek. "Maybe this is female-related. My periods aren't regular but I'm a little late—"

Oh, dear God. She was late! She could be…

No way. That wasn't possible. She looked at the two women as panic scratched inside her. "I can't be pregnant."

Peg breathed a sigh of relief. "Oh, thank God. I didn't think you knew."

"You did?" Cam blinked at her.

"I suspected. Nausea and fatigue are classic symptoms, right, M.J.?"

"Hit me hard, both times. Ben will be so pleased. He's really great with kids." M.J.'s smile was happy and excited in that way women get when a female friend is doing the most womanly thing a woman can do.

"It's not true—I can't be pregnant," she said again.

"So you didn't have sex with your boyfriend the doctor?" Peg's look was skeptical.

Cam wasn't thinking rationally enough to lie. "We used protection."

"Sweetie, if you're not on the pill…" Peg's voice trailed off and let the truth hang there.

"I'm not."

Cam hadn't trusted any man enough to let him that close so there was no reason to take an oral contraceptive. She hadn't expected that to change in Blackwater Lake. She hadn't planned to have sex. She hadn't planned on meeting a guy like Ben McKnight.

"Only abstinence is a hundred percent effective," Peg informed her. "And when a couple gets..." She hesitated, searching for the most delicate word. "Athletic, condoms can be tricky. That's why my two oldest kids have a brother six years younger."

Cam waited for her cheeks to get warm at the frank talk. She didn't remember having a discussion this personal with her own mother, but somehow didn't mind it now, with these two women. They were her friends.

"I'm going to take a wild guess here that you haven't said anything about this to Ben." M.J. took her arm and led her to the sofa.

Cam couldn't sit. "No."

Peg took the soft drink can and a glass of ice from the room service cart and poured the carbonated liquid. She handed it to Cam. "It'll be okay, honey. He's a good man."

There would be no argument from her about that. But what a mess. And maybe it wasn't true. She put her drink on the coffee table and looked at them. "Before I tell him, I think it's important to know for sure."

"Pregnancy test," M.J. said, nodding.

"If I go get one at the drugstore it will be all over town." At least here in Blackwater Lake people's behavior was predictable. Her whole life paparazzi had stalked her every move and she never knew when, where or what she'd done that would result in a horrible, incriminating picture on the cover of a magazine. She met M.J.'s gaze. "Can you get one for me?"

"Of course. There will be talk about me, but I can take the heat." Her smile was reassuring. "I'll go on my lunch hour."

"I'll make it up to you—"

"No need. It's what friends do."

"Thank you—" Her voice caught and she pressed her fingers to her lips.

"Getting emotional is another sign," Peg said helpfully.

Cam hugged the older woman, then M.J. "Thank you for being here. Both of you."

"This is just the way folks in Blackwater Lake roll," Peg said with a shrug. She pushed her room service cart to the door and M.J. opened it.

Just after the two women left the suite, the phone on the desk rang. After picking it up she said, "Camille Halliday."

"Hi, Cam. It's Glen at the front desk."

"Hey," she said, trying to sound cool and collected, as if her whole life wasn't coming apart at the seams. "What's up?"

"Your parents are here."

Her heart stopped, then started to pound. "What?"

"Dean and Margaret Halliday just checked in with me here at the desk. You look a lot like your mom," he said cheerfully.

The assumption was that she'd be glad to see them. And she was. But the timing of this surprise visit couldn't be worse.

"Where are they now?" she asked.

"They said to tell you they'll be waiting in your office."

"Understood." Her hand was shaking when she hung up the phone. "I'll be down soon."

Waiting in the office was Halliday Hospitality code for *get your tush down here as soon as possible.* That didn't give her much time to transform herself from looking like something the cat yakked up to the business professional she wanted her father to believe she was.

The thought of facing Dean Halliday Senior made her stomach drop. With the exception of a roller-coaster ride, she couldn't think of any other occasion when that was a good thing. She'd just realized that she might be pregnant.

All things considered, throwing up seemed like the sensible thing to do.

Chapter Twelve

"Mother. Dad." Cam walked into her office with a bright, phony smile plastered on her face for the parents who were seated in front of her desk. "This is really a surprise."

"I was anxious to see you." Margaret Halliday lifted her cheek for the traditional air kiss. She was blonde, blue-eyed, petite and perfect. Probably there was a resemblance until you got to the perfect part. "You look tired, Camille."

She glanced down at her designer suit and expensive heels, regretting the fact that she'd put herself together in a hurry. She also regretted that there wasn't enough concealer on the planet to hide the dark circles under her eyes. So much for plan A.

"It's been a busy few months. I'm fine." And possibly pregnant, she thought. But that wasn't something she would share until absolutely necessary. "How are you?"

"I'll be better when you give me a report on this property."

Dean Halliday Senior was a handsome man in his late fifties. His hair was dark with the exception of silver at his temples. Stray gray wouldn't dare crop up on his head to make him look anything but distinguished. If Hollywood was casting someone to play the president in a movie, Dean Halliday could be on the short list.

Cam leaned down to kiss his cheek and imagined that it was a lot like touching her lips to one of the Mount Rushmore commanders-in-chief. In all fairness, maybe her attitude toward her parents needed an adjustment. At least they were here. Then she half sat on the corner of her desk and met her father's gaze, bracing for the grilling she knew was coming.

"Things are going really well, Dad. This property could be something very special. A place to get away from it all. *Really* away, if you know what I mean."

"I do." Margaret crossed one slender leg over the other, rustling the silk of her black designer slacks. "The only airport is nearly a hundred miles away."

"Once you get here, the trip is worth it." Cam looked from one to the other. "Towering mountains. Lakes and streams so crystal clear you can see the bottom. Fresh air—"

"You sound like a travel brochure," her father said.

"If only a tri-fold glossy paper with words and pictures could adequately convey the splendor." She straightened away from the desk. "Let me show you. I'll give you a tour of the lodge."

"Lead the way." Her father stood and buttoned his dark suit jacket.

"Follow me." Cam walked out of her office and around to the lobby side of the registration desk, then looked at the blonde wearing square black glasses behind it. "M.J., these are my parents, Dean and Margaret Halliday. This is Mary Jane Baxter, one of the best customer service representatives I've ever worked with."

"It's a pleasure to meet you both." M.J. smiled, but the expression in her eyes was questioning. Did the folks know yet about the suspected pregnancy?

Cam gave a slight shake of her head, then smoothed her hair. "The staff here at Blackwater Lake Lodge is excellent. If you need anything, just let us know and—"

"How are reservations?" her father asked. "Is there an improvement?"

"Up sixty percent from this time last year," Cam said. "We're completely full for the summer and already starting to take reservations for the fall and holidays. There are even a couple of small regional conferences scheduled."

"Hmm." Her father nodded, but there was no way to tell what he was thinking. Turning away, he inspected the furniture grouping in the lobby by the stone-front fireplace. "Rustic."

His tone wasn't necessarily critical or condescending, but Cam found herself wanting to defend the lodge. "This room reflects the mountain milieu. People from New York or Los Angeles don't want the chrome, crystal and marble they see there. Here in Blackwater Lake the wood and stone brings the outdoor magnificence inside."

"Hmm." He nodded. "Let's see the rest."

"Okay. Let's go to the dining room. Amanda will want to say hello."

She led the way to Fireside and through the dining room, which was currently dark and empty of people since it didn't open until five in the evening. All the tables had linens and silverware rolled in cloth napkins. The fireplace was cold now but in a few hours flames would be dancing cheerfully. Through the double doors in the back of the room was the kitchen and that's where they found Amanda Carson.

She was about Cam's height, a beautiful brown-eyed brunette. At work she wore her long hair up in a twist and had on a white chef's coat with a single row of buttons up the front.

"I smell something burning." She sniffed and instantly the sous chef and food preparers were scrambling to find and fix the problem. "That's not the kind of smell that comes out of my kitchen."

Cam's high heels clicked on the tile floor as she walked over to where her friend stood by the long, stainless-steel work area. "Hi, Amanda."

"Cam." The chef turned and smiled. Then she spotted the elder Hallidays and moved to give each of them a hug. "I didn't know you guys were coming."

"That's because we didn't tell anyone. If you really want to know how a place is running, drop in. Advance warning gives people a chance to sweep everything they don't want you to see under the rug." Dean gave her a fond look. "How are you, Amanda?"

"Doing all right here in Mayberry." It's what she'd called the place when Cam first approached her with the deal to parlay six months into a career- and reputation-building job in the city of her choice. "Blackwater Lake is kind of growing on me."

Cam knew what she meant. The people were salt of the earth and the scenery had sort of gotten into her soul. "Tales of her culinary expertise are really bringing customers into the lodge."

"How many people could there possibly be?" Margaret asked. "This is the wilderness. Awfully far from the airport, as I was telling Camille. It took the driver forever to get here."

"It's quiet, for sure, but there's something to be said for that." Amanda warmed to her subject. "The most excitement this town has seen was when that guy checked into the hotel pretending to be—"

"Do you have the profit numbers for the restaurant?" Cam interrupted. She knew where her friend was headed with that and it wouldn't go over well with her parents. She was still trying to live down the days when she was the tabloids' favorite target. The Hallidays would probably never forgive her for that.

"I can show you the spreadsheets." The chef pointed to her glassed-in office in the corner of the kitchen. "Or you can take my word that revenue is way up from this time last year. Your daughter has really turned this place around. The staff adores her."

"It's not a popularity contest," her father said. "Sometimes you have to irritate people to run a business."

"That's the thing," Amanda said. "Cam is great at running the business and doesn't irritate anyone."

Except maybe Ben. If the pregnancy test said what she thought it was going to say, he was going to be plenty irritated. No strings attached in this bargain, he'd said. A baby was kind of a big string.

"Cam?"

"Hmm?" She looked at her friend. "I'm sorry, my mind was wandering. Did you say something?"

"Yes. You look tired."

"That's what I told her," Margaret said.

A gleam stole into Amanda's dark eyes. "Is that dashing doctor keeping you up too late at night?"

"Would that be the doctor you were kissing in the picture on the front of that horrific newspaper?" her mother asked.

Cam's chest felt tight. "I was hoping you hadn't seen that."

"Yes, indeed we did." Dean fixed his blue eyes on her and there was no warmth in them. "How did that happen?"

"I have no idea." She shrugged. "Somehow I was tracked here and the guy checked into the lodge under false pretenses to spy on me. Nothing in that article was the truth."

"What about the man you were kissing?" Margaret asked.

That kiss hadn't been for real, either. Cam hadn't felt this uncomfortable, awkward and guilty since her arrest as a teenager. "That's Ben McKnight. He's a doctor."

"Hometown hero," Amanda added. "Good-looking and smart. He likes my seven-layer chocolate cake."

"Anyone who doesn't like it would be too dense to find their way out of a plastic bag, let alone complete medical school," Dean pointed out.

Cam was pleased that the president and CEO of Halliday Hospitality, Incorporated, liked her friend's cooking, but how she wished her father had a compliment for his own daughter. She knew she'd been a pain in the neck to them for a lot of years after her brother died. She knew she'd never be as good as Dean Junior, or be able to run the business as well as he would have. But she was trying to be a Halliday her father could be proud of. Didn't that count for something?

Her best was better because of Ben, and speaking of the good doctor, she needed to change the subject before Dean and Margaret could ask more questions and trip her up, make her slip and spill the beans about their phony relationship.

"Okay, I have a lot more to show you. We'll see you later for dinner, Amanda."

"You're going to love it," she said to the elder Hallidays. "I recommend the trout. It's going to be awesome."

"You're ever the humble cook," Cam teased.

Amanda grinned. "False humility is a waste of time."

"Well said," Dean commented.

"We look forward to it, dear," her mother added.

Cam showed them every square inch of Blackwater Lake Lodge, from the large suites to the pool and extensive grounds. She saved the second-story deck that overlooked the grass, shrubs, flowers and trees for last. It was nearly noon, but the Adirondack chairs were in the shade and she urged them to sit and soak in the fresh air and view. She was surprised when they actually took her suggestion.

"I love it up here," she told them, leaving out the part where she'd used it to find her serenity when exasperated with staff who didn't take her seriously. She sat on the ottoman by her mother's chair. This was also where she'd found Ben, where he'd proposed the dating bargain. Where she'd accepted, desperate to find a way to be successful and prove to her father that she could be. All she wanted was to make him proud.

She didn't think her getting pregnant was going to achieve that objective.

"This is a very beautiful spot," her mother said.

"It is," her husband agreed. "You've done a good job with this place, Camille."

She wanted to shake her head and make sure her hearing wasn't playing tricks on her. Had the daunting Dean Halliday just given her a compliment? "We have a way to go, but things are looking up. No more hemorrhaging money. Waste has been cut and the budget trimmed in a way guests won't notice. I've hired a trustworthy accountant, who assures me that if things continue as they are, next year we'll be in good shape."

Her father nodded. "The staff looks efficient and it would show in more than the books if that wasn't the case. The grounds and public areas are well-maintained. It's a property that Halliday Hospitality can be proud of."

He'd all but said he was proud of *her*. She wanted to grin from ear to ear and maybe do a little happy dance, but that wasn't what Hallidays did. The thought of dancing made her a little nauseous and all the joy imploded.

"So tell us more about the doctor you're seeing," her mother said. "I didn't read the dreadful article. I do hope there won't be any more of that."

"I'm sure it won't happen again," she assured them.

"We're going to hold you to that." Dean put his feet up on the wooden ottoman. "Now, how did you meet Dr. McKnight?"

And so the third degree began. "We met here. He's staying at the lodge while having a house built in an exclusive luxury development that overlooks Blackwater Lake. His medical specialty is orthopedics. He grew up here in town and came back because he loves it so much."

Everything she'd said was the truth. Her parents had never been overly into her feelings, so maybe facts were enough, because defining her feelings for Ben was difficult. She was grateful for his help. She liked being with him and missed him when they weren't together. He was funny and sexy and made her heart beat faster whenever she saw him. Just thinking about him quickened her pulse. She'd never felt this way about any man. Ever.

"I imagine he'll be pretty busy during ski season." Dean looked at his wife, who nodded. "We'd like to meet him."

Her stomach dropped and when it bounced back up

there was a huge knot in it. "How long are you going to be here?"

"A night. Maybe two," he said.

"I'll notify housekeeping. There's an unoccupied suite."

"We took care of that. Our luggage has already been delivered there," her father said.

"It was a noble attempt to change the subject, though." Strangely enough, there was a twinkle in her mother's eyes. "You're not going to get out of introducing us to your doctor. We promise to be on our best behavior, right, dear?"

"No. I intend to have a word with the man who is interested in my daughter and find out *why* he's interested."

Of course her father thought it was about money, because no man could possibly be interested in her for any other reason. Of course there was a reason, but they'd never guess it. In all fairness, they had as much reason to distrust her suitors as she did. But her deal with Ben was new and different. When she'd agreed, it never occurred to her that they would have to pretend in front of *his* family, which had been hard enough. Now they'd have to do it for *hers*.

"So, will we see him for dinner?" Her mother crossed one leg over the other.

"Yes."

She'd played the part for the McKnights, and now it was his turn. It was incredibly important to keep up the pretense with her parents, especially after hearing that she was doing a good job. Now wasn't the time for how screwed up her personal life was to come out.

There was reason to believe she was pregnant by a man who was building a big house for resale, not a family. And she had taken his help and advice in order to get the career she wanted in a place that was far away from Blackwater Lake. If that wasn't messed up, she didn't know the meaning of the words.

"I'll let Ben know to meet us for dinner here at the lodge. Seven o'clock?"

"Perfect," her mother answered.

She'd do her best to keep her parents from finding out this situation was anything but perfect.

"Do you like that label, Mother?"

Cam sat on the love seat across from her parents in their suite. She'd put her own wineglass down on the coffee table and hoped now wouldn't be the time they actually noticed her. No way she wanted to explain that she wasn't drinking alcohol because she might be pregnant.

Margaret took another sip of the red. "It's quite good, Camille. A wonderful choice."

Her father was having something stronger from the suite's full bar. "This is an excellent Scotch."

"I'm glad." She smiled. "And since there was no advance warning of your visit, you know we didn't get it in just for you. No special treatment. Every guest is treated in the same special way."

"The Halliday Hospitality mission statement." He nodded approvingly. "I propose a toast."

What? she thought. No. Not that. But both of them held out their glasses, so she picked hers up. "What are we drinking to?"

"The hotel business in general, Blackwater Lake in particular. To better times ahead."

Her mother and father clinked glasses, then held theirs out to her. Her crystal wineglass tinkled when she touched theirs, but she only put it to her lips without drinking. She could fake this. It occurred to her that she was getting pretty good at faking life in general. Look at her and

Ben. They'd successfully fooled everyone into believing they were in love.

Being spotted together had required an investment of time in each other's company. She'd begun to look forward to seeing him after a stressful day at work. He actually listened to her troubles, which was better than talking to herself in the serenity place. She enjoyed his sense of humor, his smart and practical approach to problems.

If she were being completely honest, she grew breathless and weak-kneed at the sight of him and ached for him to hold her. Kiss her. Since making love to her in the mountains, he'd only touched her because they were pretending to be in love.

But for Cam it was feeling less and less like a pretense, more and more like…

"Are you all right, Camille?" There was concern in her mother's voice.

"Yes. Why?" *Please don't ask why the level of my wine hasn't gone down.*

"You had the strangest expression on your face. Are you not feeling well?"

"I'm fine," she lied. She should be getting used to it, but deceit didn't come easily to her and never would. "My mind was just wandering. I'm sorry. I was thinking about Ben."

"So, the two of you are getting serious?" There was wariness on her father's face. "I wasn't aware that something like this was part of your career trajectory."

How to answer? Cam wondered. Things were getting serious, but not in the way he was talking about. "I'm enjoying Ben's company. The reality is that I never expected to meet someone like him here in Blackwater Lake, Montana. In fact, nothing about this place is the way I thought it would be. I even went camping."

"With Ben?" her mother asked.

"A Halliday in the wide-open spaces," her father mused. "Not in a hotel."

"I know, right? That's the first time in my life that I didn't have four solid walls around me and a bathroom." But she'd been with Ben and that was enough.

Margaret glanced at the delicate, diamond-trimmed Rolex on her wrist. "Is he as handsome as the photograph on the front page of that horrible newspaper?"

"Better." Cam smiled, picturing his boyish good looks and sigh-worthy grin. "It doesn't do him justice. Pretty soon you can judge for yourself."

"Then I'm even more anxious to meet him. And it's just about time to go downstairs. I think I'll take a few moments to freshen up." She stood and went into the other room.

Moments later there was a knock on the door and her father asked, "Did you order room service?"

"No. Maybe Mother did."

"She would have said something to me."

"I'll see what's going on." She was closest to the door and went to open it.

Mary Jane stood in the hall, twisting her fingers together. "Thank God it's you," she whispered. "Your father scares the crap out of me."

"Join the club. What's up?"

"I need to warn you—"

"About?" Dean Halliday was right behind her. "Ms. Baxter, for many years I have frightened employees and I'm very good at it."

"Yes, sir." Blue eyes behind the black-framed glasses grew wide.

"Now, what is the problem?"

"Mr. Halliday—" M.J. glanced first at him, then Cam.

"There are a bunch of reporters and photographers in the lobby."

"What in the world—"

"They've been badgering the hotel staff, attempting to get quotes. As far as I can tell they're trying to support a story in which Cam—" She hesitated. "I mean Ms. Halliday—that she's in trouble again." Her voice hardened when she met the gaze of the CEO of Halliday Hospitality, Inc. "With her parents."

No. No. No, Cam thought. *Not this. Not now. Think. Problem solve.* What would Ben do?

She glanced up at her father. "We don't have to go down to the restaurant for dinner. I'll order something from room service and—"

"Absolutely not." He shook his head. "Thank you, Ms. Baxter. You did the right thing."

"You're welcome."

"And for the record?" he said. "You have nothing to be afraid of on my account."

"Yes, sir. Thank you." She smiled at him, then looked at Cam. "Call me if there's anything I can do."

"I will. Thanks. I owe you."

She closed the door. "Dad, really, I'll call Ben. He can come up the back way and meet us here."

Dean shook his head again. "Hallidays don't sneak around. We face things head-on. We don't avoid even sleazy reporters who are looking to write a sordid story about my family in order to sell newspapers."

"Okay." She decided to share Ben's wisdom after the last paparazzi ambush. "Publicity is good. Even the bad stuff. It's important to get our name out there."

"Not in those sordid papers. Not when the name is Halliday."

"Curiosity can boost reservations." It was worth one more try.

Her father looked grim. "Let's get this ordeal over with. I'll fill your mother in."

Cam watched his back as he left the room and realized that it was a terrible thing when a person lost hope. She'd been so close to getting what she wanted, so close to an assignment in Los Angeles, New York or Phoenix. Now the same seedy reporters who had ruined her life before were sabotaging the career she was moving heaven and earth to resurrect.

And then there was Ben.

He was the one she was most worried about now. This wasn't what he'd signed up for when they made their bargain. She should be glad they weren't a real couple, because it was becoming more apparent that it would really hurt when he dumped her for being constantly pursued by the press. No guy who wasn't in it to get his name in the paper could put up with this.

Now he had to meet her parents with the press photographing everything. At least she could control who else was around when she broke the news to him that he was going to be a father.

Chapter Thirteen

There was something wrong with Cam.

Ben had heard it in her voice when she'd called about having dinner with her parents. He didn't know if it was about them being here or another issue with the press.

He was sitting by the fireplace waiting for the Hallidays in the lodge lobby and it would have been hard to miss the reporters and photographers milling around and grilling the employees for dirt on the family. One of them had said to a colleague that he'd been staking out Cam's parents, just waiting for them to meet her for a face-to-face about the doctor she'd been slumming with in Blackwater Lake, Montana.

Ben had to smile at the reporter's irony. He had a heck of a nerve talking about slumming considering how the guy made his living.

Although Ben had to admit that he was a little nervous about meeting Cam's parents. Considering that their relationship was based on a mutually beneficial bargain, he shouldn't give a rat's behind what her parents thought of him. But he did care.

So far the press hadn't noticed him, but one of the reporters drew his attention. The jerk was badgering M.J. at the registration desk. She was doing her best to ignore the questions fired at her, but apparently she'd lost patience.

She raised her voice and said, "I have only one comment. Camille Halliday is a terrific boss. She's the best one I've ever had and everyone here at Blackwater Lake Lodge feels the same way."

The boss in question was just coming around the corner with a nice-looking older couple. The energy level in the lobby had been hovering in the lower register and shot through the roof when the power family was spotted. Dean and Margaret Halliday were elegant and composed as cameras started flashing and reporters hit them with a barrage of questions.

"Is Cam in a jam again? I can see the headline." The jerk held out a digital recorder.

"What do you think about her and the doctor?" another one asked.

"Is it true she's pregnant?"

"Are you here to break them up?" This guy shoved a microphone at the older man. "Care to comment?"

Ben looked at Cam's face and again knew there was something wrong. He saw shadows in her eyes and a vulnerability that made him want to protect her, to wrap his arms around her and shield her from all this craziness. She'd been putting up with it her whole life and he wondered how she'd managed to stay so sweet and strong.

He stood and pushed his way to her side through the crush of people badgering her. Standing between her and the horde who wanted a piece of her, he forced a smile.

"I'll hold one if you want to kick him."

That got a small smile. "As appealing as that would be, I'd probably just hurt myself. Besides, the assault and battery charges would just be a win for them. And it wouldn't do your career as an orthopedic specialist any good either."

"I'm getting you out of here."

He put his arm around her shoulders and led her out of the lobby. She'd told him dinner would be at Fireside and he led the way. The noise was close behind them a minute later when they arrived at the restaurant doorway.

"Do you want me to call lodge security?" he asked her.

"It's already done."

He nodded. "I went to high school with local law enforcement. Sheriff Marshall probably owes me a favor."

There was humor in her eyes. "Really? Sheriff Marshall?"

"It's catchy," he said with a shrug.

She could smile under this kind of pressure and that took guts. Ben admired the hell out of her.

The hostess was at the podium and immediately said, "Your table is ready. Please follow me."

Dean Halliday said to her, "If anyone intrudes on our privacy, I want you to call the local authorities."

"Yes, sir."

Ben and Cam looked at each other and said at the same time, "Sheriff Marshall."

When they started laughing, her father lobbed a censoring look in her direction. Ben could imagine Cam as a little girl on the receiving end of that disapproving expression for even a small infraction like fidgeting at dinner. But the rigid upbringing hadn't managed to squeeze the spirit out of her. Thank God.

They were seated in a far corner of the sparsely filled dining room, far from prying eyes. Ben held out a chair for

Cam that would put her back to the rest of the room. Even if a nosy reporter managed to get in, she wouldn't have to see and no unflattering photos could be snapped. Her father and mother were barely seated when the waiter arrived.

"Good evening, Mr. and Mrs. Halliday, Ms. Halliday. Dr. McKnight." He looked at everyone. "Welcome to Fire-side. What can I get you to drink?"

"A bottle of Jordan Pinot Noir, please, David," Cam said.

"That's an excellent choice," her mother agreed.

"I'd like something stronger," her father ordered. "Scotch."

"The best," Cam added, to the waiter.

"I'd like a beer. Whatever you have on tap is fine," Ben said.

"I'll bring that out right away. Would you like menus now or after drinks?" David was in his thirties, nice-looking and clearly knew how to provide exceptional ser-vice.

"After drinks," Cam said and her parents nodded.

Ben had a feeling she had talked to the staff here ahead of time to make sure there were no slipups in service with her parents. Probably even before she knew the press would descend like locusts.

"Well, that was unpleasant." Dean looked at his daugh-ter. "One can never live down the past, it seems."

Ben was watching Cam's face, knew the exact moment when the barb pierced her and burrowed in. Anger in-stantly ignited inside him and he couldn't let the comment go unchallenged.

"We haven't been formally introduced, Mr. and Mrs. Halliday. I'm Ben McKnight." He held his hand out across the table and one after the other they each took it. "The thing is, that unpleasantness happened because the two of you showed up here." He held up a hand to forestall her father's protest. "Not saying it's your fault, but the Halliday name brings them out no matter who's attached to it. I heard one of those reporters say he'd staked you out, just waiting for you to show up here in Montana."

The older man's eyes narrowed. "Be that as it may, Doctor, if my daughter had kept a low profile in her younger years, no one would care about the comings and goings of her parents."

"Dad, let's not do this now—"

Ben put his hand over hers and squeezed reassuringly. "The thing is that if presidents and movie stars can live down outrageous behavior and rehabilitate their images, a hardworking young woman like your daughter should get a pass on being a kid. Shouldn't there be a statute of limitations on immaturity?"

Dean opened his mouth, but the waiter arrived with their drinks and set the beer and Scotch in front of the men. Then he proceeded to open the wine deftly and pour a small amount for Cam to taste and approve.

She sniffed, then barely touched the glass to her lips. "Excellent."

"I'm glad to hear it." David filled crystal wineglasses for the ladies, then said, "I'll bring menus as soon as you're ready."

When the four of them were alone her father said, "So, tell me, Doctor, what's a guy like you doing in a small town like Blackwater Lake?"

"I grew up here."

"And what? You were homesick?"

Cam looked like she wanted the earth to swallow her whole. "Dad, please—"

"It's a fair question." Ben smiled at her, then met the other man's gaze. "This town has the very best of what the

United States of America is all about. The people take care of each other. You couldn't find a more picturesque place. The mountains offer outdoor opportunities—hiking, skiing, snowboarding. Then there's the lake for fishing and water sports."

"A great vacation spot. But for a career in the medical field, wouldn't your prospects be better in New York, Los Angeles or any other big city?"

Ben understood that this wasn't about his career as much as it was about whether or not he was after Cam's money. It wasn't bragging to let the man know he was just fine in that regard.

"I actually built a medical practice in Las Vegas and sold it for, let's just say, upwards of seven figures. Prudent investments have paid off and I don't have to work at all for the rest of my life."

"But you do. Here," Margaret Halliday interjected.

Cam's mother said "here" as if Blackwater Lake were the swamp planet where Luke Skywalker crash-landed in the second *Star Wars* movie. They would never understand, but he had to say it anyway.

"I love being a doctor and I'm good at what I do. This town and these people are a big part of the reason I've been successful in life. I wanted to give back to the community, but, believe me, I get more than I give. If the tourism industry is going to grow in this town, medical care needs to keep up."

"True enough. Cam tells us you're living at the lodge," her mother continued. The nesting questions.

"I also said you're building a big, beautiful house in an exclusive community on the lake." Cam was defending him, which wasn't necessarily part of their deal.

When Ben had proposed it, he'd never expected or intended for her to invest so much personally. He knew she was going to hear from her family later about what a low bar she'd set and didn't mind for himself. He had no emotional investment in these people, but she cared very much what they thought. He wanted to tell her parents that there was no danger of him becoming part of the family, but that wouldn't help right now. Soon she'd be gone and in her world he'd be nothing more than a blip on the relationship radar.

Oddly enough, he wanted to be more than that to her.

After dinner the Hallidays said good-night and excused themselves from the table, pleading weariness from traveling and an eventful day. Obviously that was a jab at the paparazzi and proved that they couldn't resist one more dig at the prodigal daughter. Cam should have looked relieved when they were alone in the restaurant, but strangely enough she seemed more tense.

"I know what you're thinking," he said.

She seemed momentarily alarmed. "Oh?"

"You want to kick something, and I know just the spot."

"My serenity place." She nodded. "It's been neglected lately because thanks to you, things have been going well." She sighed. "Until today."

"It happens." He held out his hand. "Let's go."

Without a word she put her fingers in his palm, then set her cloth napkin on the table. They stood and walked out of the restaurant and turned right to the exit door on the first floor. The stairway to the upper deck was right there and they took it up.

Cam settled her forearms on the redwood railing and breathed deeply. "This fresh air is just what the doctor ordered."

"Take several deep breaths and call me in the morning." *Or right now,* he thought.

Just like the first time he'd seen her in this very spot he wanted to hold her, kiss her. Now he knew how soft her skin felt, how sweet she tasted, and *perfect* didn't do her justice. Making love with her seemed like a lifetime ago and right this second he couldn't recall why having her again was such a bad idea.

When she looked up at him there was gratitude in her eyes. "Thanks for defending me tonight at dinner."

"No problem. Speaking of dinner, I noticed that you didn't drink your wine." He rested his arms on the railing and stood as close to her as he dared. Their shoulders brushed and they could almost feel the heat of the sparks flickering and flashing, then flying into the night.

She tensed and said, "I needed to keep a clear head. I'm sorry my parents were so hard on you."

"I can take it."

"You shouldn't have to. Why now?" She shook her head. "I can't believe they picked tonight to be involved parents."

"Don't worry about it. Not on my account."

But she kept going as if she hadn't heard. "Although when I think about it, the timing in every other part of my life has been a disaster, so why not this, too?"

"What disaster?" He looked down and saw a troubled look in her eyes. Then he remembered the troubled tone in her voice earlier. "What's wrong?"

She shook her head, a nonanswer. "Between my parents and the paparazzi, you must be relieved that we have a bargain and not a real relationship. The Halliday heiress and her baggage are more challenge than any man should have to take on."

It was a statement, not a question, and he didn't answer. He had a feeling that there was a lot more going on with her that she wasn't telling him. He should ask, but he wasn't sure he wanted to know.

When she'd called earlier, he'd been aware that there was something wrong without even seeing her face. He knew her well enough to tell by the tone of her voice. Knowing a woman that well could change a man forever, and Ben wasn't sure he wanted to change.

She looked up. "I think I'll say good-night. I have some things to do."

"Okay. Sleep well."

He wasn't going to.

Cam looked at the stick from the pregnancy test M.J. had brought her. It said "pregnant."

"There must be some mistake," she whispered to herself. "A false positive. It could happen."

But in her heart she knew there was no mistake, unless she counted the one where she'd slept with a man who only wanted a pretend relationship. The nausea, fatigue and her highly evolved emotional state were all signs pointing to the fact that she was going to have a baby.

Ben's baby.

She'd just left him a little while ago after standing on the deck under the stars. More than anything she wanted to throw herself into his arms and have him assure her that everything was going to be all right. But she'd sensed a distance in him. She wasn't even sure how she knew that, but he'd definitely closed himself off.

None of that changed the fact that she was having a baby. It was surreal and she couldn't wrap her head around what was happening to her.

The doorbell in her suite rang and she jumped at the unexpected sound. Ben. Part of her desperately wanted to see him. Part of her didn't. She hoped it was him come to insist she tell him what was really wrong. Then she forced herself to get real. She hadn't let herself hope for anything good since that awful day when she'd heard that her brother had been in a car accident. She'd prayed and hoped with everything she had that he would be all right, but it hadn't been enough. Dean Junior had died in spite of her hope.

She heard the doorbell again and sighed. Whoever stood there wasn't going away. If it was Ben, this was as good a time as any to give him the big news.

But when she opened the door her father stood there. "Dad. I wasn't expecting you."

"Am I interrupting?" He looked around as if there would be someone else there.

Probably anticipating Ben, since the man lived right next door. Ironically, he'd never come into her place. Neutral ground camping in the mountains was where common sense had gone out the window—and the tent didn't even have windows.

Cam looked down at her socks, sweatpants and matching zip-up cardigan. "I'm alone. Is Mom okay?"

"Fine. She's asleep. May I come in?"

"Sure. Of course. Sorry." Apparently being pregnant affected a woman's manners and basic brain function. She stepped back and pulled the door wider. "Come in."

"Thanks."

"Would you like a drink?" She looked longingly at Ben's door before closing her own. "I don't have anything here, but I can call downstairs if you—"

He held up a hand. "No. I'm fine."

"Okay." She indicated the conversation area in her suite living room. "Have a seat. It's kind of late, so I'm a little curious why you're here."

He nodded, then sat on one of the small sofas. "There's something I'd like to talk to you about."

"I'll take care of whatever it is. If there's a problem that you noticed here at the lodge, just let me know and consider it done. I have a terrific staff and we can make things happen—"

"It's not about trouble," he interrupted. "I just wanted to talk to you."

"About what?"

"I saw your employees in action with those sleazy reporters earlier. Will you give me your secret to securing loyalty like that?"

Ben. He was her secret and her strength. He'd been her conduit, the bridge to winning the hearts and minds of the workers. "The people here in Blackwater Lake are, quite simply, awesome."

"I actually want to talk about one person in particular, but there's something I need to say first." He leaned back into the cushiness of the love seat and crossed one leg over the other. It wasn't the body language of a father getting ready to grill her about the man in her life. "Your mother and I are heading back to Los Angeles in the morning."

Cam sat down across from him. "But I thought you'd be here for another day."

"I changed my mind. It didn't take as long as I'd figured to see everything I needed to see."

Was that a good thing or bad? "The lodge has turned the corner, Dad. It has the potential to be a very successful property for Halliday Hospitality, Inc. Think Vail. Aspen. Park City, Utah. The town council is investing in infrastructure so that more people will come, tourists and permanent residents both. In fact, that's why Mercy Medical Clinic wanted Ben. And they're expanding the existing clinic to provide more services. Eventually there will be a hospital here. The demographic is going to need Ben's particular skills set for the master plan—"

"Whoa." Her father laughed and shook his head. "You

had me at 'the lodge turned a corner.' I can see that from the financial reports. I'm not here to close it down."

"Good. A lot of people would lose their jobs if you did that." She was relieved to hear that was off the table. Also even more curious. "Then what did you want to talk about?"

"You've done everything you promised when you convinced me to give you a chance to prove yourself. I wanted to personally deliver the news that you're being promoted."

"I am?" Another surreal moment. She couldn't quite believe that at least one part of her life had gone according to plan.

"You can have your pick of any Halliday Hospitality property to manage." He grinned. "So, what's it going to be? Los Angeles? New York? San Francisco? Scottsdale, Arizona?"

"I don't want to push anyone out or cause someone to lose their job."

"Don't worry about that. We'll juggle assignments. No one will be out in the cold or demoted. But you've got my attention. You've earned this, Camille."

She nodded, thinking back to employee hostility and no respect when she'd arrived here at Blackwater Lake Lodge. The collective attitude of the staff and townspeople began to change when she started "seeing" Ben. And seeing him had not been a hardship—just the opposite. It had been far too easy to get used to having him in her life. She could get used to it. But now…

It was time for her to move on, just as she'd planned. She'd earned a promotion.

"Camille?" Her father looked puzzled.

"Hmm?"

"Are you all right?"

Define all right, she wanted to say. Professionally all was good. Personally? Not so much.

"Yes, I'm fine," she lied.

Dean leaned forward, forearms on knees, blue eyes intent on her. "Then why don't you look happier about this news?"

That was a very good question, because this certainly wasn't the way she'd expected to feel if this moment ever arrived, and she'd had her doubts in the beginning. When she'd talked her way into getting a chance, and that chance meant exile in Blackwater Lake, Montana, she hadn't expected to fall in love. Or get pregnant.

"I'm just really surprised by this," she finally said.

"You shouldn't be. Hard work should be rewarded. And at Halliday we do that."

"I never wanted any special treatment."

"And you didn't get any."

So spoke her boss. "Good, then."

Her father watched her for several moments, then frowned. "What is the nature of your relationship with Dr. McKnight?"

There was a loaded question if she'd ever heard one. She and Ben didn't have a relationship. All they had was a deal. Then they had sex. Now she was pregnant. All of the above would be tricky to explain in a way he would understand.

Finally she said, "Why do you ask?"

"Because I'm your father."

"Since when?"

Cam wasn't sure why she'd said that or why she wasn't horrified that she had. Maybe the baby made her do it. Whatever the reason she'd surprised her father. The expression on his face was one she'd never seen before, which meant Dean Halliday Senior wasn't accustomed to being caught off guard.

"What does that mean?" he asked.

"Tonight Ben stood up for me." And she loved him for that. There, she'd actually formed her feelings into that thought. She loved Ben. "He protected and defended me."

"From what?"

"You," she went on quickly, before rational thought stepped in to make her stop. "The press being here wasn't my fault any more than it was when they stalked me as a teenager. That was all about being the daughter of Dean Halliday, being from a wealthy hotel family." He opened his mouth and she raised her hand to let him know she wasn't finished. "I take responsibility for my bad choices in friends and the things I did. But I'd just lost my brother—"

Sadness and a grief that would never go away darkened his eyes. "I lost my only son."

She refused to back down. "When he died not only did I lose my protector, the guy who ran interference for me, I lost my father, too. You went from parent to boss, training me to be a stand-in for Dean Junior. My only qualification was being the oldest surviving Halliday heir."

"Camille, you don't know—"

"I'm not blaming you, just explaining things from my perspective. I have no idea what it feels like to lose a child." God willing she never would. "It's got to be the worst thing that can happen and I understand that you went through an awful time. But I did, too. I was sinking fast and no one noticed, no one reached out a hand." Not until she got to Blackwater Lake and met Ben. "It's okay, Dad. I finally grew up. And it just has to be said. I'll never be as good as Dean Junior would have been, but I promise to do my best not to let you down ever again."

His head was bowed, elbows resting on his knees with

fingers linked between the wide V of his legs, as if he was praying. "I appreciate that."

"Good."

He sighed and stood up. "So, you'll think about where you'd like to be transferred?"

"Yes." Then she remembered. "And wherever that is, I'm taking Amanda with me. I made her a deal."

He nodded. "A Halliday's word is more than a promise."

"All right. When do you need my decision?"

"As soon as possible." He suddenly looked tired, and a little older than when he'd walked in. "We need time to reassign personnel."

"Okay." They stared at each other for several moments without speaking, because apparently there was nothing more to say if it wasn't about business. "Will I see you and Mother in the morning to say goodbye?"

"An early breakfast?"

"Just let me know what time. I'll be there."

"Very well. Good night, Camille."

"'Night, Dad."

Without another word he left. Cam wasn't sure whether or not she felt better because of unburdening herself. She was only sad that she and her father could never have had this conversation when she needed it most. He would have told her that Hallidays don't make excuses, because they don't make mistakes.

Eventually she would have to confess to them that she'd messed up again and was pregnant. But first she had to break the news to Ben.

Chapter Fourteen

The next evening Cam called Los Angeles to make sure her parents had made it home safely. Her father informed her that the executive manager of the Halliday Hospitality Inn, Scottsdale, Arizona, was retiring and she could have the job if she wanted it. She agreed to think things over and let him know in twenty-four hours. He'd given no hint that there were any hard feelings about what she'd said to him regarding her childhood. Then again, her father was like Teflon. Things were thrown at him, but nothing stuck. Just as well.

But before she could give him an answer about the new job and relocation, she had to tell Ben about the baby. Staring at the single wall that separated their suites, she decided that putting it off any longer was just cowardly. Hallidays weren't gutless.

She was casually dressed in jeans, a T-shirt with the Blackwater Lake Lodge logo on it and sneakers. Briefly she considered putting on a power outfit, then decided against it. She was in this predicament because she'd taken her clothes *off* and no ensemble would make a difference when telling a man who'd successfully avoided commitment that he was going to be a father.

She did, however, check her hair and put on fresh lipstick. In this situation, a girl needed all the confidence she could get. With head held high and shoulders back she left her room and turned right, then knocked on his door.

A few moments later Ben opened it, saw who was there, and a slow grin turned up the corners of his mouth. The warmth moved to his eyes and for just a second there was a flicker of what looked a lot like lust.

He leaned one broad shoulder against the doorjamb in just about the sexiest pose ever. "Hi."

"Hi."

Cam's heart hammered in her chest, partly because of what she had to say, but mostly it was simply her uncontrollable reaction to this man. She lifted her hand in a small wave, then stuck her fingers in her jeans pockets. Apparently her tongue was stuck, too, because she couldn't think what to say next.

"I'm glad you finally came over."

"Oh?" She'd been tempted many times and wondered if the word *finally* meant he had been, too. But his glad reaction wouldn't last very long when she told him. "Why are you glad?"

"Word around the lodge is that your parents are gone and I was wondering how everything is." The pose got even sexier when he folded his arms over his chest. "I was going to call if you hadn't stopped by."

That was something positive, wasn't it? At least he was thinking about her. And he'd stood up to her father last night. No one had ever done that for her, not even the older brother she'd idolized. In spite of her effort to suppress it she knew hope was hovering.

"Can I come in?" Just about twenty-four hours ago her father had asked her the same thing and she'd wanted to say no. If Ben felt that way…

"Of course." He straightened out of the lazy pose and stepped back from the door to open it wider. "Do you want a beer or glass of wine?"

Her stomach dropped. Last night, out on the deck, he'd commented on the fact that she hadn't had any of her wine at dinner. Now she was here to tell him the real reason. She toyed with the idea of mentioning that he might want a drink before hearing the news, but decided not to. Looking on the bright side, it was possible the information that he was going to be a father might not produce a response that required alcohol.

"No, thanks," she said.

He closed the door and walked over to her. She was standing by the back of the love seat. His suite was a duplicate of hers, the mirror image. As he looked down, Ben curled his fingers into his palms, as if he was fighting the urge to touch her, pull her into his arms. At least she hoped… There was that word again.

The expression in his eyes grew more intense as he stared at her. "Sit. Stay awhile."

"Maybe I will." She'd really like to if this conversation went well.

"Did your folks give you a hard time about last night?" He seemed genuinely concerned. "I didn't mean to cause trouble. But none of what happened was your fault."

"I know. Dad didn't mention it again."

"Good." There was a question in his eyes. "So. I'm curious. To what do I owe the honor of a visit from senior management here at Blackwater Lake Lodge?"

"Well." She blew out a breath. "I have news. And some other news."

"Okay." He settled his hands on lean hips. "Why don't you start with the news first."

"My father is extremely pleased with my work here at the lodge."

"That's good." But the easygoing manner disappeared. "Right?"

She nodded. "He's offered me the top management position at Halliday Hospitality Inn, Scottsdale, Arizona."

"Congratulations." His voice was oddly flat. "Desert. That's different."

And he seemed indifferent to the information that she would be leaving Montana. Cam waited for more, a reaction indicating he cared even a little. It didn't happen. She supposed him asking her not to go had been a stupid fantasy, but it had been there in spite of her warning to herself.

Even so, she had no right to be disappointed. He was sticking to the letter of the agreement. He'd helped her get what she wanted and it wasn't his fault she wanted him now.

"What's the other news?" he finally asked.

It was best to say straight out what she had to say. There were no words that could possibly soften the blow. "I'm pregnant."

He looked at her for several moments, then actually laughed. This wasn't anywhere near the expected response. "You're kidding, right? It was a test. To make sure I was listening?"

She blinked back tears and double-damned the out-of-control hormones that were making her react in this hyperemotional way. When she could speak without a sob sneaking out, she answered.

"No, it's not a joke. I'm going to have a baby. Your baby." Her chin inched up slightly.

He stared at her as if waiting for her to say "gotcha." "I don't understand. How could this have happened?"

"Maybe it's time for a refresher physiology course, one that highlights bodily functions, Doctor. It's called—"

"I know what happened. I was there. We used protection."

"Yes, we did."

She remembered being really grateful that he'd had some, for all the good it had done. She'd known the risk and in the heat of wanting him so badly, she'd been willing to take that chance. She was also a victim of that natural human malady known as the it-won't-happen-to-me syndrome. Now she was just a terrible warning.

"If you recall—" She put as much primness as possible into her voice. "It was very—athletic—when we, you know—"

"Slept together," he finished.

"Yes." Although if they'd actually slept, they wouldn't be in this mess. She wanted to look anywhere except at the grim expression on his face but wouldn't let her gaze wander. "I'm told that under those circumstances condoms can be ineffective."

And that was when she realized her second fantasy of the evening had bitten the dust along with the one where he asked her not to leave. It had crossed her mind that there could be the cliché hug and twirl of happiness when he scooped her up in his arms because he was happy about becoming a father. But there wasn't so much of that reaction, either. There wasn't a speck of joy on his face, just dark looks and frowning.

"Are you sure about this?" he asked.

"I took a pregnancy test. Still have the stick if you want

to see it." She pointed at the wall separating their suites. "I can bring it over."

"Not necessary."

She knew he wanted to ask if the baby was his, but to his credit he held the words back. "Just so you know, I haven't been with anyone else."

"It never crossed my mind." Again to his credit, he sounded sincere.

She nodded. "Thanks for that."

He dragged his fingers through his hair and seemed on the verge of saying something. *Ask me to stay,* she wanted to beg him.

But that wasn't what came out of his mouth. "This is a lot to process."

Oddly enough, those were the words that broke her heart. His voice wasn't unkind and certainly what he said was true. But she'd wanted so much to hear something different.

"I know what you mean. I'm still trying to—process. But we can work something out. Visitation," she said lamely.

"Yeah." He dragged his fingers through his hair.

They stared at each other for several moments, both in shock for different reasons. Finally she realized there was nothing left to say. "I need to go."

"Right. Okay." He went to the door and opened it. "I'll call you. We'll talk."

She nodded, then walked out without another word. There was no way to speak without bursting into tears and she didn't want pity.

She wanted the fairy tale. She wanted him to love her.

Moments later, when the tears started rolling down her cheeks, she was in her own suite where no one could see her break down. Up-and-coming hotel entrepreneur heiresses didn't do this sort of thing in public. Ben hadn't intentionally lied when he'd said the bargain would keep either of them from getting hurt, but that didn't help when the pain overwhelmed her.

In her rebellious stage people had always wanted something from her. She'd thought knowing up front what Ben wanted would insulate her from feeling used. It wasn't fair, and certainly wasn't what had happened, but that didn't make losing the man she loved hurt any less.

When she stopped crying, she'd call her father and tell him Scottsdale near Phoenix was where she wanted to go. She couldn't think of a place that was more different from Blackwater Lake, and maybe a change of scenery would help her forget Ben McKnight.

"What's the holdup with this house, Alex?" Ben stood in his newly wallboarded family room and glared at his brother while their father looked on. Cam had left without a goodbye two weeks ago and every day that went by without her in it shortened his temper. She was going to have a baby. *His* baby. The news had blown his mind.

"There's no delay," Alex answered. "It's all part of the building process."

"You could have built a whole block in the time you've spent on this thing."

Brown eyes a lot like his own stared back at him, but Alex's were brimming with amusement. "Who are you and what have you done with my laid-back little brother? You remember him, right? Doctor. Easygoing. Great sense of humor. The guy who said, 'Take your time. Get everything right.'"

"Now I just want it done."

When Ben had brought Cam here the framing was complete but you could see into everything downstairs, including the garage. Now the wallboard was up, closing things off. Much like himself, he thought. And that made him angry.

The last time he'd seen her standing in his hotel room doorway, lust had hit him like a speeding train. He wanted her in his arms, in his bed, but there was more to it and he didn't think about that. She'd dropped her bombshell, then kept to their bargain and left for a better job. Just as promised, she'd packed up and brushed the mud of Montana from her pumps. And she'd done it without saying goodbye.

Ben dragged his fingers through his hair. "What's the delay?"

"There are building codes." The exaggerated patience in his brother's voice grated on already frayed nerves. "Inspectors need to examine everything to make sure it's built to those codes. After the job is done on each phase, we can't move on to the next until the city inspector signs off on the work. We have to wait."

"So can we buy this guy a drink or something and persuade him to make this place a priority?"

"Are you talking bribe?" One of Alex's dark eyebrows rose questioningly. "Because I'm pretty sure there are laws against that sort of thing."

"Might be worth breaking the law to move this project forward at maybe a pace just a tad faster than a snail's."

Tom McKnight had simply been observing the back and forth between his sons. Until now. "What's your hurry, Ben?"

His hurry was that he wanted out of Blackwater Lake Lodge. He swore his room still held the scent of Cam's skin, but that was impossible because she'd only ever been in it once. Every night of looking at the wall that had separated his room from hers made him sorry for all the missed opportunities. He regretted not going next door and kissing the living daylights out of her when he could have.

The memories were driving him crazy.

"This is about Alex dragging his feet," he said.

Tom shook his head. "Your brother is the best builder around. His reputation in California and Montana is above reproach."

"Thanks, Dad." Alex gave him a "so there" look.

The older man continued, "And you're not acting like yourself, son."

"Who am I acting like?"

"Me." His father's pale blue eyes filled with sadness. "After your mom died."

Ben couldn't believe he'd heard right and glanced at his brother. The shocked expression on Alex's face said he'd heard the same thing.

"I don't understand, Dad."

"Let me spell it out. You're acting like a damn jackass because Camille Halliday is gone." Tom's voice went hard. "The difference between you and me is that you're in a position to do something about her."

"Maybe he shouldn't." Alex was dead serious now.

"Of course he should."

His older brother faced off with their father. "In my opinion Ben dodged a bullet when she left Blackwater Lake."

"She never promised to stay," Ben defended. "It was always her plan to prove herself here then move on to a higher-profile property."

There was no reason for his father to know about the bargain. Obviously he'd pulled off making him believe he cared about her, but somewhere in the pretending he'd begun to actually *care*.

"Women are trouble," Alex continued. "Thank your

lucky stars she's outta here before doing real damage to your impressionable young heart."

Too late, Ben thought. She'd made an impression on his heart that would never go away. He was in love with her. He hadn't seen it coming, hadn't been looking for this to happen, but every night the truth hit him like cold water in the face. She was gone. The worst part was that he missed talking to her. He needed to hold her. Touch her.

"You know, big brother, just because you had a bad experience doesn't mean every woman can't be trusted."

"From what I've seen, your track record with women isn't great." Alex's mouth pulled tight. "Judy dumped you for a ski bum and went back east. Cam headed west. That only leaves ladies from north and south to put you in your place."

"Judy was wrong for him. And Cam isn't like the woman you brought here, Alex." It took some of the sting out of Tom's words when he put his hand on his oldest son's shoulder.

Oddly enough Ben's anger was anesthetized by his brother's bitterness. He'd been deceived and dumped by a woman who took away everything he'd ever wanted, everything he loved. Ben understood where he was coming from, but their father was right. Cam wasn't like that woman. She was straightforward and honest. She'd told him about the baby and he didn't say the right thing, hadn't stepped up. Being in a state of shock was no excuse. Then she'd left without a word. He'd called her, but she was dodging him.

Ben knew he'd go crazy if he didn't talk about it. He looked first at his brother, then his father. "Cam is pregnant with my baby."

"Are you sure it's yours?" Alex's eyes turned dark

and hard. Obviously he was remembering how he'd been lied to.

"I'm sure."

"Damn it, Ben—" His father wasn't in the habit of swearing, so when he did, the McKnight kids listened up. "That's even more reason not to do what I did."

"I'm not sure what you mean, Dad."

"When your mom died after giving birth to Sydney, I was angrier than I'd ever been. Mad at her."

"Why?" Alex stared at him.

"She left me with three small kids to raise all on my own. I didn't know how. She was your mom and I couldn't do it the way she did. I couldn't do it without her."

"At the risk of sounding conceited," Alex said, "you did a great job. The three of us turned out pretty good."

Tom's expression was full of regret when he looked at his oldest son. "You raised your brother and sister when you were just a boy yourself. Because you're like your mother." He sighed. "I couldn't get over her and I didn't want to try. I'm sorry I wasn't there. I'm a one-woman man and Linda was the only woman for me. And take it from me, Alex, that woman you brought here to Blackwater Lake wasn't the one."

"Doesn't matter." Alex shook his head, clearly not open to trying again any more than his father was.

"As for you," Tom said to Ben, "I don't want you to shut down like I did. You're different with Camille. Your spirit is lighter. You were happy—"

"Please don't say she completes me." Ben was going for humor but sounded kind of desperate. Because the truth was that Cam did complete him.

His dad's eyes twinkled. "When a man's been completed, he can see when it's happening to someone else. Especially when that someone is his son."

"Cam is something special," he agreed.

"So what are you going to do about that?"

"Give her time," he said.

"How long has she been gone?"

"Two weeks." It felt like two years.

"Have you talked to her?"

"I've called and left messages because she doesn't pick up. She calls back and leaves voice mail that she's fine." He shook his head. "But—"

"Yeah, but. So you haven't *talked* to her. It's been long enough." Tom's voice was firm. "Don't be stupid, Ben."

"Don't sugarcoat it, Dad. Tell him how you really feel." Alex grinned. "As fun as it is watching you call my little brother names, I've got to go. Work to do."

"What could possibly be more important than my house?" Ben demanded.

"Mercy Medical Clinic. We're finalizing all the details to start the expansion. I have a meeting with the architect. Suellen Hart. From Texas."

"A belle from the Lone Star state." *Payback time, bro,* he thought. "All big hair, sexy Southern drawl and attitude."

"Bite me." Alex scowled, then turned his back and walked away. "I'm so out of here."

Ben watched until his brother's truck peeled out of the lot, the big tires spinning and spraying dirt. He stopped laughing when he saw the determined look on his father's face. "What?"

"I'm serious, son. Camille is good people. Not only that, she's carrying your child. What are you going to do about her?"

He definitely could have handled the situation better when she'd told him about the baby, but the more he thought about it, the more he knew biding just a little time was the right thing. Somehow he had to find the words to explain to his father.

"I know waiting isn't a proactive strategy, but in this case it's the best way. Dad, her family gave her the lodge because to them it was a losing proposition anyway. She was set up for failure."

"They didn't trust her?"

Ben nodded. "She had a rough childhood and made some bad decisions, but she matured and changed. To her the lodge was a way up the success ladder, a way to prove to her family she's not that screwed-up kid anymore. The job in Arizona was her goal all along."

"Goals change. She got the job." His father frowned. "She didn't need to take it."

"Yeah, she did. That's what I'm trying to explain. She needed to know that she could follow her dream if that's what she wanted. She needed to know she was worthy. I had to let her go."

"Is this like that bird analogy? If you let it go and it comes back of its own free will—"

"Yeah. If she does that, then I know I'm her first choice."

"If she doesn't?"

"Then I'd have made her miserable by standing in the way of her trying." Ben blew out a long breath. "I love her too much to do that."

His father nodded. "Have you thought about the baby?"

"Of course. Whatever happens, my child will know me and I'll be a part of his life. Even if I have to leave Blackwater Lake and practice medicine in Scottsdale."

Tom nodded. "Okay, son. That's good enough for me. I trust your judgment."

Ben really hoped that trust was justified. When he'd first discussed the bargain with Cam, she'd wondered what would happen when she left, how he would keep the women away. He'd said he would pretend a broken heart, then come up with plan B.

He'd never dreamed his heart was in real danger, or that Cam *was* his plan B.

Chapter Fifteen

Cam looked around her new office at the Halliday Hospitality Inn. It was decorated with enlarged photos of the Grand Canyon and beautiful rock formations. The colors were Southwest-inspired—brick red, gold, beige. One wall was windows and gave her a view of Camelback Mountain and the clear blue Arizona sky. She even had a conversation area with a leather couch and chair separated by a coffee table for more informal meetings. It was big, beautiful and her heart ached because it wasn't Blackwater Lake.

There were no trees, towering mountains or grass. That wasn't entirely true, but most of the landscaping was done with rock. Very creative designs, but still hard stone. Never in her life had it occurred to her that she'd look at a pile of rocks and think landscaping. But Scottsdale was in the desert and one couldn't afford to waste water.

"Oh, who am I kidding?" She looked at her cell phone resting on the desk. It was her only connection to Ben. It was where all his texts and messages were stored, where she could hear his voice. "I wouldn't care if peanut shells were used in my yard if Ben wanted me."

A knock sounded on her office door just before it opened. Her father stood there. "Got a minute?"

"Dad. This is unexpected." She stood and moved from behind her desk. "Are you checking up on me? Have I screwed up already?"

"I just want to see if you're settling in all right." Something that looked like regret flashed in his eyes. "And I'm here because I can be. You're only a hop, skip and jump from L.A. now."

As opposed to Blackwater Lake, which wasn't easy to get to. It wasn't an easy place to forget, either.

"Is Mother with you?"

"Yes. The spa at this property is one of her favorites. She's getting some kind of facial, or massage, that involves eggplant and arugula."

She laughed. "It's probably seaweed and cucumber."

"Whatever." He waved his hand dismissively. "I heard her say something about vegetables and tuned out the rest. Don't tell her I said that."

"Mum with Mom. Got it." She tilted her head and stared at him. Who was this funny, playful man and what had he done with her father? He looked the same in his pinstriped navy suit, powder-blue shirt and coordinating tie, but this was a side of him that she didn't know.

"I didn't tune out the part where she wanted me to tell you to clear your schedule for this evening. There's a place we'd like to take you to dinner."

"There's nothing to clear because I don't have any plans." That sounded just too pathetic, but was also the truth.

"That's not good. You need a social life. All work and no play..." He shrugged. "You get my drift."

"I do." M.J. had said the same thing. "But I'm really busy right now. Still doing my homework on this property and getting up to speed. There's a lot to learn, especially before beginning construction on the new tower."

Her father sat on the couch and she settled beside him. "How are things here?" he asked.

"Not bad. Even in this slow economy we have the capital to add rooms." She crossed one leg over the other. "We get a lot of businesspeople and families on vacation. I'm going to check into the marketing campaign to see what we can do about getting more people in the door."

"You should call those friends of yours from the tabloids." He actually winked.

Now she was really weirded out. The same man who'd held her responsible for being stalked by reporters could actually make a joke about it? The world had gone mad, or maybe it was just her.

This was about business. "The employees are on their best behavior, but that's to be expected with a new sheriff in town."

Cam remembered joking with Ben about Blackwater Lake's Sheriff Marshall and then gave herself a mental shake. It was another reminder that she hadn't found the saying "out of sight, out of mind" to be true. She hadn't seen Ben for a few weeks and couldn't stop thinking about him. And the baby.

"So the place is running like a well-oiled machine?"

"Pretty much." If you didn't count the little problem she'd brought with her. Settling her hand protectively over her still-flat abdomen, she gave her father the best carefree smile she could manage.

He looked around the room. “How do you like your office?”

“It’s really big.” And very far removed from the registration desk. No M.J. right outside her door. Although she had a very efficient assistant, it just wasn’t the same.

Dean Halliday nodded his approval. “You’re doing a great job, Camille.”

And that was another thing. No one here called her “Cam.” It was either the full first name or “Ms. Halliday.” Maybe it was too soon and she was too impatient, but she missed the personal connection.

“Thanks, Dad.”

“I’m really proud of you.”

“Probably surprised, too, considering that I didn’t set a very high bar in my formative years.”

“That’s in the past. You’ve put it behind you and worked incredibly hard. I’m very proud of the woman you’ve become.”

This level of praise was unprecedented and unexpected. When he found out about the baby he’d want those words back. “I appreciate you saying that.”

“You’ve blossomed into an astute businesswoman. If your brother had lived, I don’t believe he could have done better. It’s important that you know I have every confidence in you to take over for me when I step down.”

Cam stared at her father, trying to absorb what he’d said. This was something she’d never thought to hear and, to her horror, she burst into tears and buried her face in her hands.

“What’s wrong?” He sounded bewildered and patted her shoulder.

She was just as surprised and wanted the earth to swallow her whole. “S-some b-businesswoman.”

“I meant what I said. Never expected tears and I’m getting the feeling they're not happy ones. So let me say this. You don't have to take over for me if you don't want to."

She dropped her hands and stared at him. This time she asked the question out loud. "Who are you and what have you done with my father?"

"I deserve that." He sighed. "After what you said in Blackwater Lake, I've done a lot of soul-searching. Your mother, too."

"You told Mom?"

"Yes. And you're right. We just weren't there for you after your brother died. Stupid, really. We lost one child and instead of focusing on our two surviving girls, it's like we lost them, too." Sadness made the lines by his nose and mouth deeper. "We were devastated and immersed ourselves in work. And I put too much pressure on you. When life is out of control, you control what you can."

"I'm sorry, Dad, about what I put you and Mom through."

"In hindsight I believe you were trying to get our attention. Your mom and I were just too emotionally drained to understand the behavior. I'm the one who's sorry."

"It's okay." She twisted her fingers together.

"It's not." He shook his head. "But I'll do better. And I want you to know I'm incredibly proud of you, Cammie."

The childhood nickname started the tears all over again, and this time her father pulled her into his arms.

"Tell me what's wrong, sweetheart."

"You might want to take back what you just said about being proud. I've messed up again, Dad."

"It can't be that bad."

"It is. I'm pregnant." She lifted her head and met his gaze. "The baby is Ben's, in case you were wondering."

"I wasn't." He tightened his arm around her. "I'm at a loss here. If this were business, I'd know what to do, what to say. But this is you and I've already made so many mistakes."

"You don't have to do or say anything."

"Yes, I do. I'm your father, but this is new territory. Should I ask what his intentions are? Beat him up? Throw vegetables at him?"

"It's my problem." She brushed moisture from her cheeks.

"You're my daughter and that makes it mine." He thought for a moment. "Does Ben know?"

"I told him before I left town."

"And he still let you go?"

"He was in shock."

"I know how he feels, but that's no excuse."

"He's called, but I've been avoiding talking to him."

"You have to sooner or later," he said.

"I know." So much for Halliday backbone.

Her father blew out a breath. "Do you like it here in Scottsdale?"

"Yes," she said automatically.

"Be honest. You can tell me the truth."

"Okay. I miss Blackwater Lake. I miss the town, the wilderness, the people." It was a place where someone noticed you were pregnant and bought you a test to find out for sure.

"I miss Ben."

"Do you love him?"

"Yes." She felt the tears welling again. "I guess I hoped he'd come after me."

"Okay, then. *This* I can help you with."

"What?"

"Don't be a doormat," he said. "Go after what you want."

"I don't think he wants me. Or the baby."

"Did he say that?"

"No." Not exactly, but the house he was building wasn't for a family. "But I didn't give him much chance to say anything." She met his gaze. "The thing is, at first we were just pretending to be a couple."

"What?" He stared at her. "Why?"

"Women were coming on to him. Faking sprained ankles to get his attention. It was disruptive to his medical practice and he felt the need to do something. He figured if word got out that he was dating someone, they'd leave him alone. In return, he helped me connect with the people. He grew up there. He knows the quirks, the personalities, and gave me practical, commonsense advice. More than anything I wanted to be successful there so I could prove to you I could do it. Then I'd get my dream job. So we made a bargain."

Her father thought this over, then nodded. "You wanted it badly enough to make a deal. I think I see what's going on here. Why he didn't come after you."

"Care to share?"

"Unlike me, Dr. McKnight is *not* putting pressure on you. He's giving you space. You have to let him know it's not what you want."

"But what if he doesn't want me? What if he doesn't want the baby?"

"Then he's not the man I think he is and I'll throw more than vegetables at him." His expression was hard. "But I'd bet everything I own that he cares about you very much. Don't forget, I saw him in action." He smiled. "I know it's hard, but you have to try. You might get everything or nothing, but whatever happens, you're not alone."

"Really?"

"You've got your family and we'll be there for you and

the baby." He grinned suddenly. "I'm going to be a grandfather."

"Yeah. How do you think Mom will feel about being a grandmother?"

"Over the moon. She loves babies and she loves you."

"You're going to make me cry again."

"Heaven forbid." His smile turned tender. "But I've got one more thing to say. And this is something I learned the hard way. Life is too short not to grab happiness with both hands. Ben loves you and you'd be a fool to let him get away."

"Don't sugarcoat it, Dad. Tell me how you really feel."

"Damn right." He nodded emphatically. "I haven't always been a good parent, but I'm not in the habit of fathering fools."

"Good to know. And speaking of how you really feel..." She met his gaze. "No matter what happens, I won't be taking over for you."

"It's okay." He kissed her forehead. "I had a feeling. Then I had a long talk with your sister and she'd really like a shot at it."

"Good. Leighton will do a terrific job. Thanks for understanding, Dad."

"Don't mention it. Just take care of my grandchild and go talk to that doctor."

That was her plan.

Cam drove through downtown Blackwater Lake and couldn't look at everything hard enough. Tanya's Treasures. The Grizzly Bear Diner. Al's Dry Cleaning. Even the hardware store was a sight for sore eyes. Finally Blackwater Lake Lodge came into view, with the unbelievably beautiful mountains in the distance. She felt a swelling sensation inside and figured that was just her heart and soul filling up again. After her time away, she'd been several quarts low on scenic beauty and fresh air.

And Ben.

She kept one hand on the wheel and settled the other over her belly. "We're going to see your daddy soon, little one. Hopefully he'll be happy to see us."

It had been a month and he'd continued to text and leave voice mails that had a steadily increasing note of frustration. Once she'd caught him just as he was going into surgery and couldn't talk, but the short back-and-forth made her heart ache.

Except for her parents, no one knew she was coming home to Montana because she wanted to surprise Ben. She turned right into the Mercy Medical Clinic parking lot and noticed piles of lumber and other supplies that indicated construction on the expansion was imminent. Ben would be happy about that.

She pulled her sporty little Mercedes to a stop beside his SUV. Never before had she felt such a rush of anticipation at the sight of a car. After shutting hers off, she grabbed her purse and the small covered dish beside her, then stepped out. Summer was coming and the air was warm and sweet with the scent of pine. A feeling of contentment joined scenic beauty and fresh air in her heart and soul.

Her goal was to top it all off with a healthy dose of love.

Clinic hours were over and since his was the only other vehicle in the lot, it looked like Ben was alone. Walking past his car, Cam glanced into the back and saw his backpack, obviously full. It was the one he'd brought when they camped out. Was he going into the mountains? With another woman? Judy?

Cam's chest squeezed tight as her conviction slipped. What if she was too late? Then she remembered her father's words about fools. If the window of opportunity was that small, she never had a chance in the first place.

Practicing the walk she'd planned to use, she moved to the front door and tried the knob. It was locked, so she rang the bell. She didn't know if he was angry enough to leave *her* out here, but he'd never abandon a patient. Finally the door was opened and he stood there looking too wonderful for words.

"Cam—"

"Hi, Ben."

Surprise was evident in his expression as he studied her from head to toe like he couldn't look hard enough. Then his gaze settled on what she was holding. "What's in the dish?"

"A casserole. Tuna. Cheese. Noodles. A little of this and that."

"Sounds yummy."

"So is it okay if I bring it inside?"

"If you want to." He pulled the door wide and let her pass in front of him.

"Where should I put it?"

"There's a break room in the back. It's past the reception desk. At the waiting area turn right. Go all the way down the hall. Last room on the left before the back door."

Cam had never been this nervous when she was pretending to be his main squeeze. Now she had a lot to lose. She'd missed his smile and the masculine scent of his skin. Her heart was beating so hard it was about to jump out of her chest and her legs were shaking. She wasn't sure she could pull off what she wanted to, but she would give it her best shot.

She moved in front of him and poured on an exaggerated, uneven walk down the long hall, trying to remember how it had felt after she'd kicked the railing on the second floor deck of the lodge.

She turned into the room with a table in the middle and a refrigerator. Holding out the dish she asked, "Where do you want this?"

"In the freezer." There was amusement in his eyes.

She opened the top door and saw quite a few other dishes there. "Wow."

"I'm a popular guy."

"I guess so."

He took the covered dish from her and set it inside, then closed the door and looked down at her. "Are things going well in Scottsdale?"

"Why do you ask?"

"I was sort of hoping you were having problems with the staff and came back for your serenity place."

"Arizona was fine." Her chest was so tight she could hardly talk. "The employees are extraordinarily nice and cooperative."

"Oh." He sounded disappointed.

"Why?"

"Because you're limping."

She searched his eyes for a clue that he cared for her, that she wasn't just a woman he needed a pretend girlfriend to avoid.

"You noticed that. I heard a rumor that there's a very good orthopedic doctor here who can fix what's wrong with me."

"As it happens, I am a really good doctor. Top of my class in med school and a real hotshot during internship and residency." He stared at her. "All that expertise tells me that there's nothing wrong with your leg. In fact you've got great legs and you're using them to get my attention."

"Is it working?"

"Pretty much." His eyes darkened. "Which makes me wonder why you brought food."

"You of all people should know that saying about the way to a man's heart being through his stomach—"

"Not true."

That gave her pause. Maybe she'd been wrong to hope. Maybe the calls and messages while she was away were only because of the baby. Maybe her father was right and she'd need to rely on her family's support after all.

"I noticed the full backpack in your car," she said. "Are you going somewhere?"

"To Scottsdale."

She could hardly believe it. "Really?"

He nodded. "It's been long enough. I gave you space, but I couldn't stand it anymore. I had to see you."

"Really?" Happiness flooded her.

"Yes. And if I couldn't persuade you to come back here, I was fully prepared to move to Arizona and practice medicine there."

"You would give up Blackwater Lake for—" She hesitated, wanting to say for her, but couldn't. "For the baby?"

"I want the baby very much," he said, his voice deep with emotion. "Never, ever doubt that. But I was coming after you."

"I see." She tried to be cool, but the corners of her mouth curved up. "You do realize that I was throwing myself at you just now with the limp and the casserole."

"I got it." He grinned, looking very pleased with himself.

"So I guess I gave up all the power in the relationship."

He took her purse and set it on the table, then pulled her into his arms. "You didn't give up anything because you always had the power and always will. I'm officially giving you notice that I'd like to change the terms of our bargain."

She snuggled into the warmth of him. Scottsdale had been lonely and cold, which was hard to do at this time of year in the desert Southwest. "Okay. I'm willing to negotiate."

"I'd like to propose something more permanent than our previous bargain."

"Oh?"

"Instead of dating, I'd like you to be my wife. My bachelor days are over. All the fun times filled with creative casseroles and phony limps just don't have the appeal they used to."

"I'm very glad to hear that."

"Good, because I'm not pretending. I love you. I think you should marry me and help me fill that big house with a family. Lots of kids and laughter. Make memories with me, Camille Halliday."

"That's the best offer I've ever had." Her eyes filled with tears of happiness. "And that means I'll get to stay in Blackwater Lake, which I've come to love very much."

"What about me?"

Her eyes locked with his and she willed him to see into her soul. "I love you with all my heart. Anywhere you are is home to me."

"Thank God." He pulled her tight against him and let out a long breath that sounded a lot like relief. "I was such an idiot."

"Is that so? What about top of your class in med school?"

"There I was the man. This condition called love is where I exhibited symptoms of stupid. I was so sure that dating you and having a beginning and end all planned out would control pesky emotions."

"You're not the only one. I thought knowing what you wanted up front would protect me." She pulled back a little. "Love is the last thing I expected or wanted."

"And now?"

"I wouldn't have it any other way."

Love and longing slid into his eyes. He lowered his head and whispered against her lips, "This is what I call the will-you-marry-me kiss."

His mouth settled on hers, warm and sweet in the best kiss she'd ever had. It promised love, happiness and the family she'd always longed for.

She smiled. "I would love to marry you."

And she wasn't pretending. The doctor's dating bargain was the best deal she'd ever made.

* * * * *

COMING NEXT MONTH
from Harlequin® Special Edition®
AVAILABLE JANUARY 22, 2012

#2239 A DATE WITH FORTUNE
The Fortunes of Texas: Southern Invasion

Susan Crosby

Michael Fortune comes to quaint Red Rock to persuade his cousins to come back to the family business in Atlanta. But when he meets Felicity, an adorable candy maker who owns a local chocolate shop, *she* may hold more weight than he's ready for.

#2240 A PERFECTLY IMPERFECT MATCH
Matchmaking Mamas

Marie Ferrarella

Jared Winterset throws his parents a celebratory party for their thirty-fifth wedding anniversary with the help of party planner and secret matchmaker Theresa Manetti. When he sees the sweet violinist Theresa strategically chose to entertain during the celebration, he winds up finding the woman *he* wants to marry.

#2241 THE COWBOY'S PREGNANT BRIDE
St. Valentine, Texas

Crystal Green

Cowboy Jared Colton has a dark past, and when he comes to St. Valentine to uncover some truth, he finds himself wanting to crack a different mystery...a pregnant bride who is running away from her own secrets.

#2242 THE MARRIAGE CAMPAIGN
Summer Sisters

Karen Templeton

Wes Phillips has proven his worthiness to win a seat in Congress, but does he have what it takes to win and heal Blythe Broussard's wounded heart?

#2243 HIS VALENTINE BRIDE
Rx for Love

Cindy Kirk

He loves her best friend. She, though helplessly in love with him, pretends to like *his* friend. Are they too far into a lie when he realizes that she's the one for him after all?

#2244 STILL THE ONE
Michelle Major

Lainey Morgan ran away with a hurtful secret the day of her wedding to Ethan Daniels. Now that she's beckoned to return and take care of her estranged mother, she's regretting her decision to leave Ethan at the altar. If she confronts him about the reason she fled, will he take her back?

Wild for the Sheriff

by Kathleen O'Brien

On sale February 5

Dallas Garwood has always been the good guy, the one who does the right thing...except whenever he crosses paths with Rowena Wright. Now that she's back, things could get interesting for this small-town sheriff! Read on for an exciting excerpt from *Wild for the Sheriff* by Kathleen O'Brien.

Dallas Garwood had always known that sooner or later he'd open a door, turn a corner or look up from his desk and see Rowena Wright standing there.

It wasn't logical. It was simply an unshakable certainty that she wasn't gone for good, that one day she would return.

Not to see him, of course. He didn't kid himself that their brief interlude had been important to her. But she'd be back for Bell River—the ranch that was part of her.

Still, he hadn't thought today would be the day he'd face her across the threshold of her former home.

Or that she would look so gaunt. Her beauty was still there, but buried beneath some kind of haggard exhaustion. Her wild green eyes were circled with shadows, and her white shirt and jeans hung on her.

HSREXP0113

Something twisted in his chest, stealing his words. He'd never expected to feel pity for Rowena Wright.

She still knew how to look sardonic. She took him in, and he saw himself as she did, from the white-lightning scar dividing his right eyebrow to the shiny gold star pinned at his breast.

Three-tenths of a second. That was all it took to make him feel boring and overdressed, as if his uniform were as much a costume as his son Alec's cowboy hat.

"*Sheriff* Dallas Garwood." The crooked smile on her red lips was cryptic. "I should have known. Truly, I should have known."

"I didn't realize you'd come home," he said, wishing he didn't sound so stiff.

"Come *back*," she corrected him. "After all these years, it might be a bit of a stretch to call Bell River *home*."

"I see." He didn't really, but so what? He'd been her lover once, but never her friend.

The funny thing was, right now he'd give almost anything to change that and resurrect that long-ago connection.

HSREXP0113